My Best Friend's Brother

—

The Summer I Turned Into a Girl

Natasja Eby

Gina: There is no way I could possibly say thank you for everything that you ever do for me. Personally, I don't even know why you do all those things, but I'm not complaining. Thank you, thank you, thank you.

Michelle: My inspiration, my personal motivational speaker; there really is very little I can accomplish without you.

Elijah: I love you with all my heart. Thank you for all of your support, your encouragement, your love, and for telling me to just keep writing.

Beth: Thank you for always pointing out the things that don't make sense. And I mean that in the nicest way possible.

To the rest of my family, Mom, Dad, Nathanael, Rebekka, Joel, and Rex: You know I love you all very much. Thank you for always being there for me.

PROLOGUE

"Once upon a time, there lived a king and queen –"

"In a castle?"

"Yes, in a giant castle. And they –"

"In a faraway land?"

"Yup, in a very, very far away land. Now this king and queen were getting old, and they thought –"

"Were they pretty?"

"Pretty? Yeah… sure. The queen was very beautiful and the king was as handsome as any king ever was. Now, shhh…" Colin put a finger to his lips and smiled at his younger sister, Cassidy. Cassidy made a gesture like she was pulling a zipper across her lips and then smiled back at him. "Where was I?"

Cassidy un-zipped her lips and said, "The king and queen were getting old."

"Oh yeah," he said. "They were getting old, which is a natural thing, of course. But it worried them because they had no heir. But then an amazing thing happened."

"What?"

"Just when they'd lost all hope, they had their first child, a son," Colin said with a grin. "So you can imagine how happy they were to have a prince in the kingdom."

"What did they call him?" Cassidy asked.

"Uhh... Christopher," Colin answered. "But that's not all. A year later, they had another baby! A girl this time."

"A princess!" Cassidy exclaimed. "What was her name?"

"Sophia, princess of light and... music," Colin answered.

"Was she pretty?"

"Of course. Even prettier than the queen, they say."

"Colin?"

"Yes?"

"I want to be a princess."

Colin smiled. "You *are* a princess."

"Princess of what?" Cassidy asked.

"Princess of... light and music."

ONE

"Cass!" Colin yelled through the bathroom door. "Exactly how long does it take you to do your stupid hair?"

"My hair is *not* stupid!" came Cassidy's shouted reply, muffled by the barrier between them. "And it'll take as long as it takes."

Colin sighed audibly, and then when there was no response from Cass, he sighed even louder. She knew how much he hated waiting for her. She knew how impatient he got whenever she had to get pretty just to go out anywhere. He didn't even want to go out, but their mother was making him accompany Cass and her friend Jessica to the mall. And he hated going to the mall even more than he hated waiting for Cass to be ready.

"Are you two ready?" Mrs. Jacobs called from downstairs.

"I'm not going, Mom," Colin called back, fed up with Cassidy's antics.

"Of course you are," Cass said, sweeping out of the bathroom at that very instant. "Don't be silly, Colin. We'll have a great time."

Cassidy's dark hair was pin-straight and her make-up was even and practically without flaw, a testament to the hour she'd spent on her appearance. While her hair, hazel-green eyes, and olive-toned skin were a perfect match to Colin's, that was about the extent of their similarities.

"*You'll* have a great time," Colin sulked.

"Kids!" Mrs. Jacobs called again.

"Come on," Cass said, grabbing Colin by the wrist and pulling him behind her.

Colin pulled free of Cassidy's grip, but he knew it was pointless to argue. Even though Cass was now fourteen years old, their parents still made Colin go with her to the mall. Maybe they did it because they knew the only reason Cassidy and Jessica went to the mall together was to talk about boys, look at boys, and waste money. Mr. and Mrs. Jacobs should have found this counter-intuitive, since Colin always ended up leading them straight to all of his male friends. However, they never seemed to know about *that* particular part of the mall trips.

Cass called, "Shotgun!" and took the front seat before Colin had even gotten his shoes on.

He got into the back of the van, letting out another heart-wrenching sigh of disgust.

"We're picking up Jess, too, right?" Mrs. Jacobs asked.

Cassidy bobbed her head up and down and enthusiastically replied, "Yup!"

Colin groaned behind them. Jessica was even more annoying than Cass was, in his opinion. She had always struck him as being one of those pretty but extremely flighty girls who was about as a shallow as a puddle on a concrete sidewalk. And yet, his own sister and parents treated her like one of the family.

Cass turned around in her seat and gave Colin an inquisitive glare. "Do you ever consider brushing your hair?"

Colin glared back. "For one thing, I *comb* my hair. And for another thing, someone was hogging the bathroom, so I didn't exactly get the chance to do it. So yes, I consider it. And yes, I do it."

"Rarely," Cass muttered.

"I think you mean when I get the chance," Colin threw back. "Which, because of you, is rarely."

"Kids…" their mother said in a warning tone.

"Sorry," Colin and Cass said in a uniformly unapologetic tone.

After a few minutes of driving, Mrs. Jacobs pulled into the driveway of the Lewis home. Jess was already outside, waiting for them on the porch swing. She was wearing a pink sundress and a summer breeze caught her blond highlighted hair as she made her way to the van. Jess smiled through the windshield at Mrs. Jacobs and Cassidy, and Colin realized with horror that she would have to sit next to him.

Jess opened the other side door, tossed her purse on the floor next to Colin's feet and sat down, neatly tucking the skirt of her dress beneath her legs. Colin nudged her purse over with his foot and Jess rewarded him with a frown. She took the purse and placed it gently next to her sandaled feet.

"Hey, Cass," Jessica said. "Hi, Mrs. Jacobs. Thanks so much for the ride."

"Oh, no problem, sweetie," Mrs. Jacobs said, smiling at her in the rear-view mirror.

Colin rolled his eyes. His mom always called Jess a 'sweetie' and for the life of him, he could never figure out what was so sweet about her. She turned her smile in his direction.

"Hey, Colin."

Colin grunted in response.

Jess shook her head. If Cassidy weren't her best friend, she would never *ever* keep company with Colin Jacobs. There was something about him that really irked her. He was just so cocky and obtusely annoying. And if it weren't for the fact that all of his friends were cute athletes, she wouldn't bother hanging out with them either.

Colin scowled and she realized she'd be staring. She answered him with an icy smile that was anything but sweet.

"What's with your brother today?" Jess asked Cass as they made their way through the mall. Colin was trailing behind at a bearable distance.

"Oh," Cass waved a hand, "he's all uptight because I took longer than he liked getting ready. And he hates the mall or something."

Jess cast a glace back at Colin. "Poor guy," she said in an unconvincingly sympathetic tone. "Has to spend his day doing something fun. I really feel bad for him."

Cass giggled. "It's so hard to have fun sometimes. Especially for him."

Jess laughed along with Cass. "Seriously though, we should find a way to cheer him up. Or at least something to take the perma-frown away."

"Hey, I think I know just the thing!" Cass exclaimed. She pointed to a group of their friends who were sitting at a couple of the tables in the mall food court. "Colin!" she called to the sullen boy behind her.

"What?" he answered back in his characteristically unimpressed tone.

She waved him forward and when he had joined her and Jess, she said, "I found some of my friends. Come sit with us."

Colin looked over in the direction that Cass was pointing. There were five girls crowded around some tables, all dressed alike and seemingly talking at the same time. Inwardly, Colin groaned. There was nothing he'd like less than to sit with Cass and Jess' chatty friends and pretend like he was having a good time.

"Um, actually," Colin said, halting in his steps, "you guys go ahead. We can meet back here in an hour."

"But Colin, I promised Mom I'd help you back-to-school shop," Cass said. She looked impatiently back at her friends who were starting to wave them over.

"So I'll buy a shirt and pretend like you picked it out," Colin said.

Jess snorted. "Your mom'll never believe that. You have horrible taste in clothing."

Colin glared at his sister's friend. "So buy me a shirt then, Jess!" he gritted through his teeth. "Then we won't have to pretend."

"Dude, calm down," Jess said, holding her hands up in surrender.

"Yeah, be nice," Cass said. She eyed her friends again. "We'll meet you back here in an hour."

Without another word Cass moved toward to the group of girls. Jess trailed behind her, shooting Colin a lingering look over her shoulder that said "get over yourself." Colin rolled his eyes and walked away in search of something better to do with his time.

One of the girls, Ashley, pulled over two more chairs for Cass and Jess to sit in. "Was that your brother?" she asked, as she retook her seat.

"Unfortunately," Cass said with a groan.

"He's cute!" Jennifer, another girl, said.

"If you like the sulky, boring type," Jess muttered.

"Are his friends around?" Gina asked. "Tenth graders..." She sighed.

"Um, for one thing, this is my brother we're talking about," Cass said. "So, ew. And also, I don't know if Colin even has friends."

The girls laughed with her, but Cass felt a momentary twinge of regret. In a way, she supposed she was Colin's friend, but ever since he had started high school, they had started drifting apart. He used to like to spend time with her, but now he was obsessed with sports and hanging out with other sporty people.

Cass forced herself back into the moment while Jess was saying, "And then he's all like 'so buy me a shirt!'" The girls giggled again.

"We totally should," Gina said. "That would be hilarious."

"We're not buying him a shirt," Cass said, trying not to snap at them. "Can we just talk about something else?"

"Geez. Sorry, Cass," Jen said with a touch of defensiveness in her voice. "Didn't realize it was such a touchy subject for you."

"It's not," Cass muttered.

Jess glanced over at her best friend's face, noticing that something was clearly wrong. She looked back at the other girls. "Hey, did you know that Bluenotes is having like a massive sale?" she asked.

"I totally already bought three shirts from there," Gina said with a huge smile on her face.

Gina started to pull out the items from her bag as Cass sent Jess a thank-you smile. Jess always seemed to know when to bail Cass out. That was what best friends were for, after all.

After Colin left the girls, he headed in the opposite direction of the food court. The giant new Sport Chek was waiting for him. It was the only thing he'd ever be interested in seeing at the mall, and an hour would give him plenty of time to look at everything.

This year, he knew he'd need a new pair of skates. He'd had an epic growth spurt over the summer, and the skates he had wouldn't cut it for the hockey season. But it was something he could put off for a few months. So he went instead to the soccer section to find some cleats. Last year at school, he'd decided to try football. This year, he thought he'd be better suited for soccer. Football was still too physical for his admittedly smaller-than-other-guys frame.

"Hey, hey, hey," Colin heard from behind his right shoulder.

Colin turned around and smiled at his friend, Ian. "Hey! You're back from camp."

"Yup," Ian said. "Got back yesterday."

Colin grunted his response and studied Ian. He looked different. His blond hair was now even blonder, and his light skin had darkened from countless hours in the sun. And as much as Colin hated to admit it, it looked like Ian had toned up a bit. Ian's physique was a sharp contrast to Colin's lean body.

While Colin was mentally comparing himself to his friend, Ian was going on and on about his sports camp, and how much fun it had been, and how he'd made so many friends. Ian followed Colin all the way to the check-out, and kept up his stories while Colin bought his cleats. Colin tried to find a lull in Ian's speech so he could extricate himself from the conversation, but Ian wasn't letting up.

Finally, Colin looked pointedly at his watch and said, "Oh man. I'm sorry, I really have to go. I told my sister I'd meet her like... five minutes ago."

"Oh, Cass?" Ian said with a dazed expression on his face. "Man, your sister is like... *so* pretty."

Colin grimaced and started walking away. "Um, well anyway, I have to –"

"I mean, *super* pretty," Ian continued, following Colin out of the store. "Like, if I saw her right now, I'd ask her out."

"Cass?" Colin asked in surprise. "I doubt she'd go for it."

"Sure she would," Ian said. "Yeah, and you can take her friend out, too. We'll make it like a double date."

"Not in a million years," Colin said with a defined tone of disgust in his voice.

"Okay, well… let me know if you change your mind," Ian said. "I'll catch you later, Col."

"See you at soccer practice," Colin answered to Ian's retreating back.

On the way home from the mall, Colin was granted the front seat so the girls could sit in the back and chat. Jess pulled out a few of the new clothes she'd bought to show Mrs. Jacobs in the rear-view mirror.

"Did you have a nice time at the mall, Colin?" Jess asked in a teasing voice.

Colin crossed his arms and slumped lower in his seat, but didn't dignify her question with an answer.

When they stopped at Jess' house, she got out, dragging five bags with her, careful not to let anything drop on the ground.

"Did you get all of them?" Cass asked.

"Yeah, I think so," Jess said. "Thanks again for the ride, Mrs. Jacobs. See you later, Cassy." She gave Cassidy a big smile which Cass returned with one of her own.

Jess went straight up to her bedroom, eager to lay her new clothes out on her bed so she could decide which outfit to wear on her first day of high school. She smiled as she reached into her last bag. Then her smile slipped as she looked at the shirt she pulled out. It was a boy's shirt, the one that all of the girls had pitched in to buy for Colin as a half-joke. It was supposed to have gone with Cass.

9

Jess sighed. She supposed she would have to go there and give it to him. Judging by the clock on her wall, she figured she still had time to walk over to the Jacobs' house and get back before supper.

When Jess got to their house, there was no car in the driveway, but she tried the door anyway. It was unlocked, so she let herself in.

"Hello?" Jess called. "Cass?"

"She's not here," came Colin's voice from the kitchen. "Who's that?"

"Who's that?" Jess mimicked, walking into the kitchen with one hand on her hip. "What exactly happened to your manners?"

"Oh, it's you," he said with disdain. He turned back to the toaster he had been fiddling with and said, "Cass and Mom went back to the mall to return one of the shirts Mom hated."

"Okay, well I just came to drop off…" Jess let her sentence drop as she watched Colin reached for a butter knife from the drawer. "What are you doing?"

"Nothing," he said, trying to block her view of the toaster. "Just whatever it is, you can leave it on the table."

"Is that a butter knife?" Jess asked, frantically tossing the bag with his shirt on the kitchen table. "That doesn't look safe…"

"I know what I'm doing, Jessica," he said. "There's just something stuck inside, that's all."

"Are you crazy?" She went to the counter to watch over his shoulder as he attempted to stick the knife into the toaster. "Are you *trying* to kill yourself?"

"Back off," he tossed over his shoulder.

"No! You're going to hurt yourself!"

Jess leaned over and grabbed the hand that was holding the butter knife. He tried to shake her off, but she wouldn't let go. In his effort to get Jess to let go of him, he thrust his hand out and the knife made contact with the inside of the toaster. There a sharp snapping sound and sparks flew out of the toaster as both Jess and Colin were thrown back by a zap of electricity. Then everything went black.

TWO

Jess groaned deep in her throat and put a hand to her forehead, her fingertips still tingling where the electrical current had travelled through her body. She opened her eyes to the blinding light of the overhead ceiling lamp and then shut them tightly again.

"Ughh, Colin you're an idiot," she said. Her voice sounded weird to her and entirely too low. "Wha…?"

Jess sat up just in time to see … herself across the room! Her eyes widened and all the blood drained from her face as she watched her own body stumble forward.

"Jess…" Colin said. "Whoa, what happened to my voice? I sound like y –"

Colin met his own eyes staring at him in utter horror, and screamed at the same moment Jess did. Jess pulled herself up using the help of the counter, while Colin scrambled around, trying to navigate standing in a dress.

"What is this?" Colin screamed in horror, putting his hands up to his newly acquired breasts.

"Don't touch those," Jess hissed.

Colin dropped his hands as he suddenly realized what he was doing. "What happened to us?"

"You were being an idiot and now," Jess looked down at her body – *Colin's* body – and shook her head, "I'm a boy! This is bad. This is so, so very bad."

"This isn't bad! This is horrible," Colin said. "I don't want to be in your body!" He picked up the butter knife off the floor and started toward the toaster.

"What are you doing?" Jess asked.

"I'm going to try to switch us back," Colin said. "Come here, hold this knife. Ugh, how do you girls walk in dresses?"

"Colin, that's what got us into this mess in the first place," Jess said, firmly grabbing the knife and pulling it away from Colin. It was surprisingly easier than Jess had expected and she ended up pulling so hard that she was thrown back a bit.

"We have to at least try, Jess," Colin said. He held out his hand but Jess didn't move. "Before Mom and Cass come home. Seriously, they can't find us like this."

Jess hesitated but finally conceded his point. She let Colin take hold of the knife too and together they pushed it into the toaster. Nothing happened.

"Maybe if we turn it on?" Colin suggested, his voice sounding more timid through Jess' vocal cords.

"Yeah, no. I think the only thing worse than suddenly being inside your body would be to die in your body," Jess said irritably, pulling the knife away. "What are we going to do?"

"I don't know," Colin said, his voice sounding even weaker. "But... ugh, I feel like I'm going to throw up. Why do I feel like throwing up?"

Jess' face went bright red. "I'm... *you're* having... my period," she said quietly.

But Colin could still hear her. "I'm what?" he shouted, outraged.

"I'm sorry," she said. "It's not my fault! It's you, you did this to us." Then, without warning, Jess burst into sobs.

"Aw, Jess, please," Colin said in an unsympathetic tone. "Anything but that. Don't cry."

12

"Don't cry?" Jess said between sobs. "I'm a boy. I don't want to be a boy."

"Do you think I want to be a girl?" Colin asked in a barely controlled voice.

"It's better than being a guy," Jess mumbled.

"Better?" Colin asked, now thoroughly angry. "Better how? I feel like throwing up and clawing your eyes out, and you think this is better than being a guy?"

Jess' only response was another sob and more tears. She sat down onto the floor, folding her knees neatly underneath her. With a sigh, Colin came to sit next to her with his knees up, not caring that the skirt of the dress fell down.

Colin gripped his stomach and heaved in a long breath. "How can you stand this pain?" he asked wearily.

Jess sniffed and wiped the back of her hand across her cheeks. "Just try breathing deeply. And I'm sure Cass has some Midol or something around."

Colin shook his head. "Can't see why she would." When Jess gave him a strange look, he explained, "She hasn't had her period yet."

"What?" Jess asked softly. Colin's only response was a moan as he clutched his stomach harder. "You're lying," Jess said, her eyes narrowing.

"I'm not lying," Colin said. "Why would I lie about that?"

"But… Cass never said anything," Jess said.

"Exactly," Colin said. "Trust me, I know. Even if she spends more time with you, she still lives with me."

"What's that supposed to mean?" Jess asked, feeling angry all over again.

"I just meant –"

"That 'oh, someone else decided to be nice to my sister, and now I'm all jealous.' Is that what you meant, Colin?" Jess interjected.

Colin glared at Jess, anger flaring through his mind. "How come I have to deal with the pain and yet *you're* PMS-ing?"

Jess stood up abruptly and yelled, "Just shut up and give me my body back!"

Colin also stood, though he was still feeling queasy and answered back, "I would if I could, believe me!"

Just then, they heard the front door of the house open. Colin and Jess stared wide-eyed at each other, internally debating what they should do. Should they explain what had happened to them? Would anyone even believe them?

Jess took a glance at the clock on the stove and groaned. Picking up a banana, she said to Colin, "Here, eat this and go to my house. I'll hold down the fort for now, but we really need to meet later tonight to figure this out."

Colin took the banana in a confused stupor and whispered, "I can't go to your house like this."

"You have to," Jess whispered back frantically. "My grandparents are coming over for dinner."

"But –" Colin could hear Cass and his mom coming toward the kitchen.

"Okay… invite me and Cass to dinner," Jess said, thinking quickly. Colin just shook his head. "Please, Colin, we need to make this work."

Just then, Mrs. Jacobs and Cass stepped into the kitchen, both surprised to find Colin and Jess standing there. Finally, Colin shook himself from his daze.

"What's going on?" Cass asked, her eyebrows drawn together.

Jess stepped toward the table and picked up the bag. "Jess just came to give me this great shirt you girls bought me. Thanks," she said awkwardly.

"Oh, I forgot about that. Thanks, Jess," Cass said.

"A shirt?" Mrs. Jacobs asked. "Go try it on, Colin."

The blood drained from Jess' face at the thought of having to redress Colin's body. "Uhhh," she hesitated. "Maybe later."

Colin stepped in at that moment and said, "Hey, Cass, my grandparents are coming over. Do you and… Colin want to have dinner with us?"

"Me *and* Colin?" Cass asked sceptically.

Jess smiled to try to make it seem like that was an idea that should have sounded completely natural. Obviously by the look on Cass' face, she wasn't buying it.

"Well, that is sweet, Jessica," Mrs. Jacobs said with a grin. "You both should go. It would be nice for you." Her decision made, Mrs. Jacobs left the three teenagers in the kitchen.

"*Really?*" Cass asked.

"Yeah, when was the last time the three of us had a nice dinner together?" Jess asked.

"Never!" Colin answered with a fake giggle.

"Exactly," Jess said, shooting Colin a warning glance.

Cass raised an eyebrow and looked back and forth between her best friend and her brother. "What exactly happened here while I was out?"

"Nothing!" Colin and Jess replied in unison.

"I just wanted to bring over that ridiculous shirt," Colin said with a smirk.

Jess smiled tightly and added, "And then she stopped me from accidentally killing myself."

"O… kay," Cass said, obviously less than convinced. Then she shrugged. "Whatever. Come help me pick out an outfit for dinner, Jess."

When Cass turned to leave the kitchen, Jess motioned Colin forward. Colin raised his eyebrows and pointed at himself, the silent question hanging in the air. Jess nodded and, with pursed lips, pushed Colin forward. Colin stumbled a little, threw one last glare at Jess, then followed Cass to her room.

"Sorry about Colin," Cass said as she entered her room and shut the door behind him.

"For what?" Colin asked more defensively than he meant to sound.

Cass' brows drew together slightly before she answered, "Oh you know him… He's always being kind of jerky."

"Oh…" Colin said, not sure how to respond to that. "He was okay today."

"Really? That's not what you said earlier."

Colin tried not to frown too deeply. What had Jess said about him earlier? That he was a jerk or something? Why would she think that? They weren't best friends, but he hadn't done anything mean to her lately.

Cass started pulling different coloured shirts, skirts, pants and dresses from all orifices of her bedroom. Colin hadn't even known that Cass owned all of that clothing, but he begrudgingly said yes or no to whatever she showed him. And then, to his great horror, Cass started to undress. Colin turned around abruptly, trying to hold in his scream of horror.

"Jess, what's wrong?" Cass asked in concern.

"Nothing," Colin said without turning around. His worst nightmares were all coming true and he couldn't even do anything about it.

"Well, what do you think of this?" Cass asked.

Colin turned around slowly, relieved to find her fully dressed. Of course, he couldn't tell what the difference between her new outfit and her old outfit was, nor did he care. So he shrugged, and hoped that would mean that she looked fine.

Cass looked at herself in the mirror for a couple minutes and then said, "Nah, I think I'll put the other shirt on."

She started pulling her shirt off, and Colin slapped a hand to his eyes.

"Are you okay?" Cass asked. "Seriously, what's wrong?"

"I uh… I have a headache. It's really bright in here. Can I turn the light off?" Colin flicked the light switch without waiting for an answer and added hastily, "Thanks."

"But I –"

"You look great. Let's go," Colin said.

"I'm not wearing a shirt," Cass answered, sounding a little testy. "And I can't see."

Colin didn't answer. A moment later, there was a shuffling sound, then the light flicked back on. Cass quickly pulled on another shirt and headed for the door.

"I don't know what's up with you, Jess," she said. "But let's go."

"Let's get Colin," Colin said.

"You sure you want to bring him?" Cass asked.

"Yes!" Colin answered a little too eagerly.

"Oh alright, but I'm not responsible for anything he says or does," Cass said.

"You never really were," Colin mumbled as Cass knocked on his closed door.

"Coming!" Jess called in a sing-song voice that Colin didn't even know he had.

When Jess opened the door, Colin nearly stumbled backward in surprise. Jess had dressed Colin's body in black dress pants, a crisp, navy, button-down shirt and had even added the only tie he owned to the ensemble. Cass' eyebrows shot up in surprise.

"We're not going to a funeral, *Colin*," Colin said, his eyes wide.

"I know. It's just dinner with your grandparents, but I thought I should look my best," Jess answered sweetly. "Don't you think so, Cassidy?"

"Sure," Cass answered uncertainly. "I mean, you look really nice, Col. I'm just surprised."

As Cass led the way down the stairs, Colin whispered to Jess, "You dressed me in *that?*"

Jess leaned down and whispered back, "I wasn't going to let you meet my grandparents looking like a slob."

"I have other clothes," Colin said, careful not to let Cass hear their conversation.

"I didn't exactly have time to iron. Or do laundry," Jess shot back. "We're going to be late as it is."

Colin rolled his eyes, but kept silent. As they walked to Jess' house, he had to walk next to Cass and leave Jess trailing behind them so that Cass wouldn't suspect anything was amiss. However, that also meant that he had to listen to his sister's pointless and boring stories.

"So when I went back to the mall, I saw him again," Cass whispered.

"Saw who?" Colin asked, trying to feign interest.

"Shhh," Cass said. She looked back at Jess, who smiled at her. Lowering her eyebrows, she added, "Ian."

"Ian?" Colin asked too loudly.

"Yeah," Cass said like it was obvious. "And he looked so good today."

"What, do you have a thing for him?" Colin asked, trying to mask the sound of shock in his voice.

"Oh, Jess, you're too funny," Cass retorted. "But I thought we already decided it was more than just a thing."

"Oh, yeah, of course," Colin said, reeling inside at what he'd just learned. "But I didn't think you... still liked him."

From behind them, Jess could hear everything they were talking about, but she tried to make it look like she couldn't. Inwardly though, she was freaking out because she knew how much Cass would hate it if Colin found out about her crush.

Luckily though, Cass just laughed it off, saying, "You're in such a weird mood today, Jess."

"You could say that again," Colin answered.

Jess was relieved to find out that they had beaten her grandparents to her house. She slyly motioned for Colin to let them in, which Colin awkwardly did.

Before Jess walked into the house, Colin stopped her and said, "Can I talk to you a sec... Colin?"

Jess met Cass' confused eyes for a brief moment before saying yes.

"We'll be right in," Colin said to Cass, shutting the door and leaving her in the house alone. He turned back to Jess, but hesitated to ask his question.

"What is it, Colin?" Jess asked. "Cass is going to be suspicious."

"It's just…" Colin sighed heavily. "I still kind of feel like throwing up."

"Oh," Jess said, her voice laced with sympathy. "Go up to my bedroom, and in my night table, you'll find some medicine. It'll make you feel a lot better."

"Thanks," Colin said. But when he didn't move to open the door, Jess' look of concern changed to questioning. "How are we going to do this?"

"Just… try to be me. At least for today," Jess said.

"Well, then you have to try to be me," Colin said. "Which means you can't dress like this after today."

"I'm hoping I won't have to worry about that," Jess said. "Let's meet tonight after everyone's asleep. I want my body back."

"I know," Colin said, chewing on his bottom lip.

They stepped back inside and as Colin made his way up to Jess' room, Cass said, "You guys were out there for a long time. What did Jess say to you?"

"Oh, you know," Jess said, forcing a careless shrug. "She was all like 'My grandparents are really old-school, so try to have some manners.' And I was like 'Okay, whatever.'" Jess tried to mimic the tone of voice that Colin would have used, and judging by the look on Cass' face, it worked.

"Well you should try to be good," Cass said. "It was nice of her to invite you here too, so just… behave."

Jess tried not to laugh out loud at the irony of the whole situation. Instead, she said, "It was nice of her, wasn't it?"

Colin came back down and led Jess and Cass into the dining room. Colin had only really been inside Jess' house once or twice, so it was a struggle for him to make navigating her house look natural. Thankfully, Jess' parents greeted him like the daughter they thought he was. They seemed surprised to see Jess there, who they, of course, thought was Colin. But since he was Cass' brother, they didn't seem to mind, and they set out an extra place for her.

When the doorbell rang and Jess' parents went to answer it, Jess took the opportunity to lean down and whisper to Colin, "I call them Grampy and Gran-Gran. Don't forget."

"Okay," Colin whispered back, irritated.

"And *please* be kind to them," Jess added.

"Geez," Colin said, resisting the temptation to glare at her. "I know how to act around old people."

Jess rolled her eyes, but before she had a chance to answer, her parents and grandparents had entered the kitchen. Her Gran-Gran smiled brightly at Colin and kissed his cheeks noisily, while her Grampy eyed Jess warily.

"Hey… Gran-Gran," Colin said uncertainly.

"What's all the whispering going on in here?" Grampy asked gruffly. "Is this your boyfriend, Jessie?"

"No!" Jess, Colin and Cass all answered at the same time.

"Of course not," Colin said.

"Nope, just friends," Cass added.

"Barely friends," Jess agreed.

Grampy eyed them suspiciously, then shrugged with a "Let's eat!"

Colin and Jess both sighed in relief at her grandfather's apparent acceptance of their answers. They tried to keep silent during the meal, only giving minimal answers when they were asked anything. Neither of them was eager to be the other person, but they knew they'd have to suffer through it, even for just a little while.

Finally, dinner ended and Jess' grandparents went home. Cass said goodnight to Jess' parents and made her way to the front door. Neither Colin nor Jess moved. Cass looked back at them and gave them a weird expression.

"Colin," Cass said. "Come on."

Jess snapped out of her reverie and came to stand with Cass. Cass then moved to hug Colin goodbye, but he side-stepped her. When Jess glared at him, he laughed it off as a mistake and then stepped into Cass' embrace like he should have in the first place.

"Bye, Cass," Colin said, trying to make his voice sickly sweet like Jess would have. Then he cast a brief, bewildered gaze at Jess.

Thinking quickly, Jess pulled Colin into a tight hug and whispered into his ear, "Meet me at the park tonight. We have to figure this out."

"Fine," Colin said. "Let me go, Cass thinks we're crazy."

Jess pulled back and smiled awkwardly. "Okay, we can go home now, Cass."

Just as Colin was closing the door on Jess and Cass, he heard Cass say, "You're so weird, Colin."

"You have no idea," Colin murmured after he shut the door.

THREE

As soon as Colin shut the door, he could hear Jessica's mother calling over the sound of water running into the kitchen sink. It took Colin a moment to realize that she was calling him, and finally he reacted and found her in the kitchen.

"Uh… yeah?" Colin said as he entered the kitchen.

Mrs. Lewis chuckled. "The dishes won't do themselves, Jessica."

"Oh." Colin scanned kitchen, looking for any signs of a dishwasher, but there were none. No dishwasher at all. He couldn't imagine how they could possibly get along without a dishwasher in their house. And then he met Mrs. Lewis's eyes and her face told it all. There was a dishwasher, and its name was Jessica.

Mrs. Lewis tilted her head in the direction of the sink and said, "Come on, I filled up the sink for you."

Colin suppressed a sigh and plunged his hands into the scalding hot water as Mrs. Lewis walked away. He immediately withdrew them, the shock of the temperature making him feel paralyzed. He wondered if Jess did this every single night, hand-washing all of the dishes in what felt like fire. While her hands might have been used to it, his mind wasn't. Who in their right mind hand-washed dishes anymore anyway?

A few streets away, Jess wasn't having a much better time. She'd already listened to Mrs. Jacobs complain that she – or rather *Colin* – hadn't raked up the grass clippings after mowing the lawn today and how she would have to put out the garbage. When Jess asked for Cass' help in putting out the garbage, Cass snorted in derision.

"Seriously, Colin?" Cass retorted. "I still have vocal exercises to work on. Plus that's always been *your* job, remember?"

"Oh… right," Jess responded.

Jess fumbled around the garage, pulling out all the recycling and garbage. She thought she wouldn't be able to manage the two large garbage bags, but she quickly learned that Colin's body was surprisingly stronger than it looked and certainly stronger than Jess' own body was. Somehow, it felt exhilarating to be able to do so much work and not even feel tired after. And it almost excused that fact that taking out the garbage was solely Colin's job.

When Jess was done, she went into Colin's room and shut the door, not knowing what else she should do. In the next room over, Cass was doing her vocal exercises. She'd always thought that Cass had a pretty voice whenever she sang, but at the moment she sounded a bit like a dying cat. It wasn't at all the pretty voice that Jess was used to hearing. But maybe that was what it took to do the kinds of things that Cass did with her voice.

Jess looked around Colin's room. It was a mess, as she'd expected. Clothes were strewn around the room; from his bed, to the chair at his desk, to the over-flowing drawers of his dresser, and falling off of the hangers in his closet. Jess grunted in disgust. As long as she was here, she figured she might as well do him a favour and clean up a little.

Of course, that involved smelling each piece of clothing to determine its cleanliness, folding things, re-hanging things, picking up old pieces of pizza from under Colin's bed, clearing away cobwebs and ancient popcorn, and finally making Colin's bed. Which Jess suddenly realized she might actually have to sleep in tonight if they couldn't get back into their own bodies. The thought made her shudder. She changed the sheets in case she had to come back that night.

Finally, when everyone had settled down for the night, Jess silently snuck out of the house and made her way to the park that was between hers and Colin's house. He wasn't there yet, so she sat on a swing. Or at least she tried to sit on a swing and ended up cramming Colin's hips between the two chains while the seat creaked beneath her weight.

That was where Colin found her; hunched over on a swing in his body, digging her toes into the sand. He had approached her from behind and silently sat in the swing next to her so as not to startle her. Jess' body settled easily into the swing.

"Wow," Colin said. "It's been such a long time since I could actually sit in these."

"I noticed," Jess said dryly, but her voice held a hint of sadness as she studied the boy-turned-girl next to her.

"How do we get back?" Colin asked quietly.

"I don't know," Jess said, even sadder than before. "But I don't want to stay like this. I can't. There's too much..." A sob cut off her sentence.

"I know, Jess," Colin said, trying to sound reassuring. Jess' voice made it easier for him to sound sympathetic. "I don't really want this either."

"I mean, I haven't even gone to the bathroom," Jess continued like Colin hadn't said anything. "I just feel too uncomfortable in your body."

"Wait – you haven't even peed?" Colin asked, getting up from the swing to stand in front of her. "How can you do that to me? That's my body!"

"Well, come on... what did you expect?" Jess asked. "I – I can't."

"I have done awful, disgusting things for *your* body, and you won't even let mine *pee*?" Colin asked in horror.

Jess didn't answer, and as Colin stared her down, her bottom lip began to tremble and tears started slipping down her face. He sighed.

"Please, not the water works again, Jessica," he said, offering her his sleeve.

Jess pushed his hand away and whined, "You think I'm disgusting."

"No… no," Colin tried to negate her. "It's not you I find disgusting, it's your body."

At that comment, Jess started crying harder. Colin smacked his forehead and then reached forward and took her hands – his hands – her hands.

"Okay, I didn't mean it that way," Colin said softly. "I'm just not exactly used to being a girl, Jess. You have to believe I didn't say that to make you feel bad."

Jess sniffled and looked up at him. "What do we do?" she said in a whisper. "I have a dance recital in a few days. How am I supposed to dance in your body?"

Colin's eyes widened. "No! No, you absolutely cannot go prancing around in my body."

"It's not prancing around, Colin," Jess said defensively.

"Not to mention," Colin added, "that there's no way I can do a soccer try-out in… in this!"

"*This?*" Jess stood up and grabbed Colin's arm. "This is mine; I want it back."

Jess pulled her own body forward so hard that she and Colin knocked foreheads. They both fell back with the force, holding their heads and groaning in pain.

"Well that didn't work," Colin squeaked out.

"Colin, I'm so sorry," Jess said, crawling over to him. "Are you okay?"

Jess reached out to him, but he pushed her away. "This body is so fragile," he said with more sympathy than contempt. "I mean, how do you do it?"

"Colin, can you please focus, here?" Jess said in exasperation. "We have to change back."

"How, Jess?" Colin asked, sitting down cross-legged.

Jess sat opposite him, folding her legs beneath her. "Think. There's gotta be –"

"I don't know!" Colin shouted. "What am I supposed to think about? My one idea was to electrocute ourselves and you didn't like that idea. So now it's your turn."

Jess stared at Colin, shocked at his outburst. "I was only trying to... to help. I don't want this anymore than you do," she said softly.

"I know that," he answered, trying to calm down. "I just don't know what you expect from me."

She sighed. "Well it's obvious we're not getting our bodies back tonight."

"I don't know how or if we ever will," he said in a defeated tone of voice.

"Well, we shouldn't just give up," she answered him, trying to sound optimistic. "Maybe... maybe we can talk to our parents."

Colin snorted derisively. "And tell them what? 'Jess and I got electrocuted and now we're in each others' bodies?' Yeah, that'll go over well."

Jess silently acknowledged Colin's logic. She knew deep down that no matter how convincing she and Colin were, no one would ever believe they'd switched bodies. It was a hopeless case.

"We still can't give up," Jess repeated. "Listen, in the meantime... tomorrow morning, you have to tell my mom that you're not feeling well and see if she'll let you stay home instead of going to dance rehearsal."

"Fine," Colin said. "The truth is, I'm not feeling well, and even if I felt great I wouldn't go to your stupid rehearsal."

Jess barely quelled a bout of anger she felt rising inside her. "This isn't about you not being able to dance or wanting to. It's about me looking like I can't dance."

Colin threw his hands up in irritation. "Yeah well, I have soccer practice tomorrow. What are you going to do about that?"

"Same thing you're going to do," Jess answered. "Tell them I'm ill, and get out of it."

Colin shook his head. "That won't work, Jess. Men don't take sick days, especially not for sports. You pretty much have to be dying."

"You're hardly a man," Jess muttered.

"Well, you're less of a man than I am," Colin retorted. "Look, you have to go, okay? If I miss a practice…"

"Oh, what? They'll kick you off the team?" Jess asked half-jokingly.

"I wouldn't even make the team," Colin answered quietly, not meeting Jess' eyes.

Jess gazed into Colin's sincerely remorseful face. She rolled her eyes, shook her head at the ridiculousness of the situation and finally said, "I don't know the first thing about soccer."

Finally Colin looked up at her, the corners of his mouth twitching. "What's there to know? Just kick the ball if it comes to you and fake it until I figure out how to get my body back."

Jess thought about it. Kick the ball and fake it. How hard could it be, right? "If I do this, if I go to your practice… will you go to my rehearsal?"

"Do you really think that's wise, Jessica?" Colin asked. "I mean honestly? Do you want me to show up there and make you look like an idiot in front of everyone?"

Jess was pretty sure Colin meant that he just didn't want to *feel* like an idiot in front of everyone, but she didn't mention it. "It'll be fine, Colin. Just follow the other girls and… fake it," she said, throwing his words back at him. When he didn't respond, she added, "It's only fair."

Colin pursed his lips and said, "Fine. A practice for a practice."

"*Rehearsal*," Jess corrected.

"Okay, whatever. A practice for a rehearsal. Then we switch back, no matter what it takes."

Colin stuck out his hand, and Jess shook it. For one day they could be nice to each other. But just for one day. Colin stood and tried to help Jess up, with surprising difficulty.

As they left the park, Colin asked, "Do you want me to walk you home?"

Jess looked Colin up and down, mentally admitting that her body now seemed much frailer than Colin's body felt. She chuckled. "Do you want *me* to walk *you* home?" she asked back.

Colin looked down at himself and laughed. "Nah, I think I'll be okay." When they were about to split ways, he said, "Hey Jess – do us both a favour. Go pee when you get home."

"Will do," Jess said, mock saluting him. Although the idea still made her feel uncomfortable.

FOUR

Jess' alarm went off at 6:30 a.m. next to Colin's head. He glanced at the clock and groaned, suddenly remembering that he wasn't quite himself anymore. It also occurred to him that if he were in his own body, he'd be getting up at 8:00 for soccer, not 6:30 for dancing.

Dancing. Of all the things he could have done that morning, he had to go dancing. He didn't even know what kind of dance Jess did, but he sure hoped it wasn't something crazy like tap-dancing.

He soon found his answer as he went to Jess' closet for something to wear. In the garish light of day, her room was even girlier than Cass'. There were posters upon posters along the walls, most of them ballet-themed, some of them featuring male actors that Colin would never be able to name. What little paint could be seen under them was light pink. The fuzzy carpet, that Colin admitted to himself was rather nice to walk on, was hot pink. And the impossibly tiny ballet shoes hanging from the closet door handle were a faded dusty rose.

Colin picked up the shoes, wondering how he'd ever get his feet into them. Of course – they were Jess' feet. He looked down. Nope, they still looked too big for the shoes.

"Jessica!" Mrs. Lewis called from outside the door. "You can't be late, honey."

"Uhhh…" Colin hesitated. "Yeah, just getting dressed."

"Well, hurry," she said. "I've got your shake ready."

"My shake?" Colin asked, more to himself.

Mrs. Lewis heard and replied, "Yes, your breakfast shake, Jess. If you don't hurry, you'll have to sip it in the car."

Sip it in the car? "Okay, just hang on a sec," Colin answered back.

He started flipping through Jess' closet, but the only things in there were some frilly dresses and shirts that looked like they belonged in a magazine. He checked the dresser instead, hoping to find some shorts or sweatpants or something. What exactly did one wear to a ballet practice? Why hadn't Jess told him any of this? Finally, he found a drawer that seemed to be home to some sort of comfortable workout clothes. Those would have to do.

As soon as he left the bedroom, Mrs. Lewis shoved a tall glass of sickly green slop into his hand, giving his clothing choice a raised-eyebrow once-over. She shook her head and then ushered him quickly to the car. Colin sipped the gunk only twice; he didn't have the stomach to handle any more than that.

Mrs. Lewis left him in front of the town's recreation complex, a building Colin knew existed but had only seen once before. He had no idea where to go for the practice. He glanced at Jess' mom, but she was already driving away. He looked back at the building. He'd have to find his way in somehow.

After aimlessly wandering the inside of the building a few times, a janitor finally stopped him in the middle of the hall he was cleaning and asked if he was alright.

"I'm just..." Colin's face flushed. "I'm a little disoriented," he said, not wanting to admit that he was lost. "I'm going to be late for my ballet practice."

"The dance room's just down the hall," the janitor said. "Last room on the left... but you knew that."

"Of course," Colin answered, forcing a nervous laugh. "I just... I'm having an off-day."

The janitor nodded, but didn't answer. He went back to sweeping the floors, and Colin nervously made his way to the dance room. When he opened the doors, a flurry of girly girliness met his gaze. There were about a dozen teenaged girls talking and laughing as they warmed up.

Some of the girls were hanging on to a bar and stretching their arms. Others were sitting on the floor, spreading their legs further than Colin thought anyone's legs should ever be able to be stretch. And a couple of the girls were making graceful arches with their arms as they perfected their moves in perfect unison.

Colin suddenly felt overwhelmed. In general, he was fairly confident, comfortable in his skin. But now of course, he was in Jess' pasty white skin and he didn't have a clue what to do. As he looked around the room, he recognized Ashley and Jen. He didn't know whether to feel relieved or horrified that he was about to make a fool of himself in front of people he barely even knew.

Of course, all these girls knew Jess and they all greeted him. He said hi back, knowing that it was too late to make an escape. Ashley and Jen waved him over, and he silently cursed Jess for getting the better end of the deal. He sat next to where the girls were stretching and finally came face to face with the ballet shoes.

"What's with the yoga pants?" Ashley asked, reaching down to touch her toes and turning her head toward Colin. Ashley, like most of the other girls, was wearing leotards and leggings.

Colin tried not to let his surprise show at Ashley's contortionist act. "I just wanted to be comfortable," he told her. He went back to the complicated issue before him.

"Um, do you need some help, Jess?" Jen asked, folding herself down in front of him.

He tossed the first shoe toward her. "Fine," he said irritably.

Ashley sat next to Jen and took the other shoe. "Is everything alright?" she asked softly.

"Just having a rough day," Colin answered cryptically. At least it was the truth.

"It happens to the best of us," Jen answered as she squeezed Colin foot into the shoe.

Ashley repeated Jen's action and nodded sagely. "Yup. You just relax, girl. Dancing will make it all better."

Colin didn't know whether to be touched by their concern or to scream in pain as they tightened the laces of the shoes. Pursing his lips, he kept all his thoughts to himself. Finally, with each shoe done, Ashley and Jen stood as one and then reached down to pull Colin up. The action felt rehearsed and Colin wondered how many times these girls had had to pull Jess up off the floor.

The dance instructor clapped her hands and all the girls started toward the centre of the room. Colin walked – or rather, stumbled – along with the rest of the girls. They all seemed to instinctively know that they should form a circle, so Colin tried to edge his way into it when he realized that was what they were doing.

The instructor led them in some simple stretches and Colin was surprised to find that some of them were similar to the ones he did before soccer practice. Of course, he would never admit that to anyone, especially not Jess. Still, it made the first part of rehearsal a little better than he expected.

After that, though, Colin was a mess. First of all, they didn't dance to music. They danced to the instructor shouting, "One! Two! Three! Four! Five! Six! Seven! Eight!" over and over. Secondly, Colin had no sense of rhythm when it came to matching the steps the other girls did with the number being called. And lastly, he discovered that he was just plain bad at dancing. Which would have been embarrassing enough without the instructor calling every once in a while, "Pick it up, Jess!"

When the torture was finally over and everyone went back to stretching, Ashley and Jen came over to Colin and gave him pitying looks. He shrugged it off, but they obviously cared too much about Jess to let it go.

"You really are having a bad day, aren't you?" Ashley asked.

"You have no idea," Colin murmured.

"Hey, we should go grab some milkshakes," Jen suggested. "That'll make you feel better."

Colin perked up at the idea. He loved milkshakes, but he had always been lactose intolerant. Jess' body, on the other hand, could handle milk just fine as far as he knew. He smiled.

"That sounds like a great idea," Colin said in all truthfulness.

Jess was jolted awake by some heavy metal music coming from a clock-radio next to her. Gasping, she hit the snooze button and checked the time. 8:00 a.m.? How could that be? That meant she was really, *really* late for – Jess' thoughts were cut off abruptly by some caterwauling coming from somewhere outside her room. Except it wasn't caterwauling – it was just Cass doing vocal exercises again. And this was Colin's room.

Jess pulled back the covers and sighed. Yup… she was still in Colin's atrocious body. And then she remembered her agreement with Colin, which meant that she had to go play soccer that morning. She just hoped that Colin had held up his end of the deal.

Luckily, Jess remembered seeing some soccer clothes last night while she was cleaning. She retrieved them and pulled the clothes on, wrinkling her nose. They weren't anything like her beautiful dancing clothes, and she had no idea when Colin had last cleaned them. She made a mental note to throw them in the wash once she got home.

Cass walked by just as Jess was opening the door. Cass peered in briefly and then did a double-take, her eyes wide open.

"Hey, Cass," Jess greeted.

"Whoa, what happened to your room?" Cass asked, ignoring the greeting.

"What do you mean?" Jess looked back at the room with a frown.

"It's… it's got a floor!" Cass said in mock surprise as she entered the room to see it better. "Still smells, though. Seriously, Colin."

And just like that, Cass had swept out of the room and down the stairs before Jess could even defend herself. Then again, she had to admit that Colin's room did smell. But there wasn't much she could do about it now. She had to get to soccer practice.

Down in the kitchen, Mrs. Jacobs had set out a heaping plate of eggs, bacon and toast for Colin. Which, of course, Jess would be eating. She eyed the plate, trying to hold back her disdain. What she wouldn't give for one of her mom's breakfast shakes at that moment. Instead, she had to eat Colin's breakfast so as not to raise suspicion.

Jess had only taken one slow forkful of eggs when Mrs. Jacobs said, "Eat up, Colin. You're going to need that energy if you want to make the team."

"Make the team?" Jess mumbled through her eggs.

Mrs. Jacobs chuckled. "You feeling alright, son? The team is all you've been talking about since school ended."

Jess swallowed hard. Was Colin's admission to the soccer team really that dependant on whether or not Jess played well today?

"Yeah, of course," Jess said, more to herself than to Colin's mom.

"Well, hurry up and eat," Mrs. Jacobs said. "You know Coach doesn't like it when you're late."

In response, Jess shoved a few more forkfuls of egg into her mouth, took a bite of toast and ignored the bacon. "I'm ready," she said.

"You sure?"

Jess nodded, even though she wasn't really ready. She had been telling Colin the truth last night when she said she didn't know the first thing about soccer. His response – "kick the ball and fake it" – wasn't much help either. She didn't know how to kick a soccer ball. A pirouette she could manage. But kicking? It was like the opposite of every smooth, graceful, lyrical move she'd ever learned.

When she and Mrs. Jacobs pulled up to the high school's soccer field, Jess' apprehension turned to dread. Twenty or so boys were already stretching, running, and kicking balls back and forth. Jess put her hand on the door handle and hesitated.

"Have fun, Col," Mrs. Jacobs said.

"Thanks," Jess mumbled as she stepped cautiously out the door.

As she walked toward the other boys, some of them waved to her and greeted her. The only one she recognized was Ian, and he was avidly trying to get her attention. Maybe if she weren't in Colin's body, she'd be revelling at the fact that she was surrounded by so many older boys. In this case, however, she wasn't quite so eager.

"Colin, my man," Ian said when she reached him. "I want to do a couple laps. Come with me."

"Okay…" Jess said hesitantly. She didn't really want to run anywhere, but she figured she had no choice, so she got into a running position.

Ian lifted an eyebrow at her. "You should really stretch a bit first."

"Of course!" Jess said.

She should have known that. Any sort of physical activity required stretching before and after. She stretched her legs out, dissatisfied when they didn't go as far as she was used to stretching. But then, this was Colin's body. Who knew what he did with it when he was at practice.

Ian watched her for a couple minutes and then finally asked, "What kind of stretching is that?"

Jess stood up straight. "It's umm…" *don't say dancing, don't say dancing.* "It's just something new I learned. Really good for the knees."

Ian nodded, apparently approving her unconventional use of unfamiliar warm-ups. Then he started running and Jess took off, trying to catch up to him. When Ian saw she was far behind, he slowed up until she was level with him.

Although Ian kept silent as they jogged around the track, it was obvious that running was a social thing for guys. A couple of the others joined in behind them. Jess didn't necessarily enjoy jogging, but she found that it was at least not as hard as she thought it would be. Apparently Colin's body was more suited to running than Jess' was.

Later, Jess found out why it was so important to run around before actually playing a soccer game. After Coach had assigned shirts and skins – Jess gratefully accepting a shirts position – he blew his whistle and everyone got into their positions. Jess had no idea where she was supposed to go until she saw a position open in the middle of the field and everyone staring at her to take Colin's place.

As soon as Jess was in position, Coach blew a whistle and suddenly there was a flurry of action, during which all the guys ran around after that stupid black and white ball. Jess couldn't make sense of any of it. She tried to run after the ball, but Coach kept yelling at her to keep position. Well, that didn't make any sense to her, since everyone else went every which way.

Then Coach started yelling at Jess to get the ball "once in a while." Jess once did have the ball, but didn't kick it quickly enough before one of the skins guys took it away from her. Another time, the ball was passed to her, and she kicked with all her might – too soon to realize she was kicking in the wrong direction.

"Jacobs!" Coach boomed across the field. "Sit! Radcliffe, you're in!"

When Jess realized that Coach was referring to her, she left the field and gratefully sank down onto the bench off on the side. The guy who replaced her was even scrawnier than Colin was. And watching him, Jess could tell he wasn't very good. So for a moment, she regretted making Colin look *that* bad on the field, when she was sure he must have been much better than that.

And then she remembered that she never would have been in this position in the first place if Colin hadn't been messing around with that stupid toaster. Jess crossed her legs and her arms and scowled at everyone on the field. This wasn't her place, it wasn't where she belonged and she had no reason to succeed here.

"Wow, Col, that was rough," Ian said when practice was over.

"Yeah, well…" Jess didn't have an answer for him.

"You're going to need to step it up if you want to make first string," Ian added. "Come on, let's go."

"Go where?" Jess asked suspiciously.

"To get burgers. Where else?" Ian replied, giving her a weird look.

"Burgers?" Jess didn't do burgers.

"Yes!" Ian said in an exasperated voice. "DQ. Burgers. Milkshake for me, Arctic Rush for you. What's up with you? We did this every week before I went away to camp. Did you already forget?"

"I…" Jess hesitated. "I guess I did forget. Sorry."

Jess and Ian walked from the school to the Dairy Queen up the street. When they got in, Jess was shocked to find Colin hanging out with two of her best friends. And it even looked like he was having a good time. At that moment, Colin looked up at her, and instead of looking apologetic, he smiled. Jess rolled her eyes. Those were *her* friends he was hanging out with.

FIVE

Colin tried not to let it show that he was embarrassed to have been caught having a good time with Jess' friends. Ian wouldn't care of course, since he thought Colin was Jess. But for Jess to catch him at it was weird. Of course, finding himself in a girl's body was weird enough to begin with.

As Jess and Ian waited in line to order, Ian said, "Hey, those are your sister's friends, right?"

My friends, Jess wanted to say. Instead, she simply nodded.

"Your sister's not here, though?" Ian asked in a hopeful voice.

"No, she doesn't dance with them," Jess responded.

"Oh…" Ian said disappointedly.

"Why? Were you… hoping she'd be here?" Jess asked, starting to feel that there was more to Ian's line of questioning.

"Nah… I don't know," Ian said. "I kind of like her, you know?"

"You do?" Jess asked, sounding more excited than she'd meant to.

"Is that… okay?" Ian asked.

"That's great!" Jess said. "I mean," she shrugged in what she hoped was a nonchalant way, "that's cool, I guess."

Oh, she couldn't wait to tell Cass. Cass would be so excited to hear it. But… No, she couldn't tell Cass, not like this. Cass would hate it if she thought Colin was the one to tell her. She would think that Colin was teasing her. No, that wouldn't do. Jess would have to get Ian to tell Cass himself.

"Oh, we're up next," Ian said, and the conversation was over.

Colin watched in horror as both Jess and Ian ordered milkshakes. Ian gave Jess a strange look and then shrugged. As they turned away from the counter, Colin waved anxiously to get Jess' attention, but she was ignoring him.

"Hey, Ian!" Colin called, standing up. Ashley and Jen stared at him wide-eyed but he didn't care. "Colin! Come sit with us."

As Ian nudged Jess in their direction, Ashley whispered, "What are you doing, Jess?"

"Just catching up with some friends," Colin answered.

Jen snorted. "So Colin and Jocky McJock are suddenly your friends?"

"Yeah, why not?" Colin said irritably. Before Jen had a chance to respond, Ian and Jess had reached their table. "Colin, is that a milkshake?"

"Yes," Jess said with a slight narrowing of her eyes.

"But... you're deathly allergic," Colin said. "Do you really think that's wise?"

"I wanted to tell him," Ian said with a shrug as he took the seat next to Colin. "Last time he had a kids' cone, he was spewing for like... twenty minutes."

Jess' face twisted into disappointment. So not only was Colin hanging out with her friends, he was also enjoying the fact that she wasn't allergic to milk. Great. She sank down into the seat next to Ashley.

"I guess I was... overcome with temptation," Jess offered.

"Do you want me to buy you an Arctic Rush or something, Colin?" Ashley asked with a huge smile.

"Sure..." Jess answered uncertainly.

"I'll just take that," Colin said, reaching for the shake.

"Uh, no you won't," Jen said, moving it out of Colin's reach. "No more than one a week. We all agreed."

"Wha –"

"In that case, I'll take it," Ian said. When he grabbed the drink, no one argued with him. Not even Colin, who was now about as disappointed as Jess was.

"Dancing, ladies?" Ian asked, by way of making conversation.

"Yup," Colin answered.

"We have a big recital coming up," Jen informed them.

"Oh yeah?" Ian answered. "When's that?"

"This Friday at three, actually," Ashley answered as she sat back down and passed Jess the icy drink she'd bought. "You guys should come see it." She smiled sweetly in Jess' direction.

"That sounds really nice," Jess said, smiling back at her.

"Except that we have soccer try-outs that day," Ian said with another classic shrug. "Sorry, ladies."

Jess and Colin looked up at each other in startled surprise. They were both thinking the same thing: would they be able to switch back in time for the recital and try-outs? If they couldn't, they were both in some hot water.

"I guess…" Jess swallowed hard, "I guess I can't make the recital then."

Colin nodded slowly. "Not unless something changes…"

Colin and Jess decided to walk each other home, even though it was a long way away. They figured they needed the time to think things out. Like how they were going to get back into their own bodies before Friday.

"There's no way I can do your recital," Colin commented after they'd walked in silence for a while.

"Who said anything about doing my recital?" Jess asked in shock.

"No one," Colin answered calmly. "I'm just saying, there's no way I *could* do it, even if I wanted to."

Jess snorted. "Like you'd want to," she said sarcastically.

Colin thought about it for a moment and then said, "I suppose ballet wouldn't be that bad if one were good at it."

Jess stopped and put her hands on her hips, staring at Colin. But Colin just kept walking and saying, "I mean... your body is, like, so limber... Hey, where'd you go?" He turned around and met her startled gaze.

"Colin, you're being really creepy," Jess admonished.

"What are you talking about?" Colin asked, crossing his arms at her.

"Telling me my body is so," she rolled her eyes, "limber? Honestly?"

"Well, it's true!" he said, throwing his hands in the air.

"So? That doesn't mean you say that stuff out loud," she informed him. "I mean, do I go around telling people how strong you are for how skinny you look? No!"

Colin's lips curled into a half smile. "You think I'm strong?"

Jess immediately flushed. "That's not –"

"Yes it is." Colin's half-smile was now a full-fledged smirk.

"Okay, fine. Yes, you're stronger than your scrawny little body would imply," Jess threw at him. "Happy?"

"I don't know," he said, his smile fading. "I can't tell if that's a compliment or an insult."

"It's a simple observation," she said. "Don't look too deeply into it."

"In that case, don't look too deeply into me telling you that your body is limber," he told her with a shrug. "A simple observation."

"Fine."

"But seriously, I've never been able to bend the way you can!" Colin exclaimed, just for good measure.

"Colin!"

Colin just laughed and ran away as Jess chased him down the sidewalk. But Colin's years in soccer training didn't help him get very far away from her. In fact, it accomplished the opposite of his goal, since Jess now had all of Colin's strength and speed. Jess caught up with Colin and, surprising him and herself, grabbed him by the waist and picked him up.

"Jess, let me down!" Colin yelped in an unsatisfyingly high-pitched voice. He struggled against her arms, but unfortunately, Colin's body really *was* stronger than it looked.

"No 'til you apologize," Jess said, secretly laughing at Colin's plight.

"For what?" he asked, his voice rising higher and higher.

"For disrespecting my body," she said.

"Um, I think *you're* the one disrespecting your body at the moment," he pointed out.

"Whatever," Jess said, lowering Colin to the ground. When he spun around to face her, she added, "Just don't go around saying creepy things."

Colin rolled his eyes. "Don't go around abusing your new-found… superpowers."

"I'd hardly call these superpowers," Jess said, pointing to his arm muscles with a smirk.

"Oh, *such* a gentleman," Colin tossed at her with another eye-roll.

As he started walking past her, Jess said, "And you're just a perfect lady, aren't you?"

Colin stopped walking momentarily to do a sloppy curtsy, and then both he and Jess dissolved into laughter. Their laughter released the tension that they'd been feeling since the switch. And suddenly, everything didn't seem so bad. But that didn't exactly settle the matter of what would happen if they couldn't switch back.

"So what are we going to do?" Colin asked quietly.

Jess sighed. "I don't know," she admitted. "I mean… today I discovered I'm terrible at soccer. There's no way I could do your try-out."

Colin chewed his bottom lip in thought. "But... I can't do it either, Jess. Not like this," he gestured down at himself.

"And do you expect me to do a recital like this?" Jess answered in frustration.

"Well... it's Saturday. So we have about a week to figure out how to change back, or..." Colin let his sentence hang.

They fell silent again. Colin automatically steered them in the direction of his house and Jess followed without thinking. Neither of them was willing to admit a deeply ingrained truth – that they could very well be stuck like this. Forever.

"Maybe," Jess started hesitantly, "we could help each other out."

"What do you mean?" Colin asked suspiciously.

"Like... if you teach me to play soccer, and I teach you how to dance..."

"That's a crazy idea, Jessica," Colin said, not bothering to hear the rest of her sentence.

"Why is that so crazy?" Jess asked in an offended tone of voice.

"Because it took a long time for me to learn to play soccer that well," Colin answered. "And I'm sure you've been dancing since you were born or something. We would never have time to learn all that stuff."

"Hmm... actually that's a good point," Jess said.

"Exactly."

"My *body* knows how to dance," she continued on. "All you'd have to do is remember the steps."

"What? That's definitely the opposite of where I was going with that," Colin mumbled.

"Colin? Don't you think I could use what your body knows, too?" she asked in a hopeful voice.

"Yes, I guess you might be right," Colin said. "My body would know how to play soccer... if you knew what you were doing with it."

"Then teach me!" Jess said excitedly.

"Really?"

"Really."

Colin pursed his lips and then finally cracked a smile. "You're really up to learning soccer?"

"If you're up to learning to dance. *With* elegance and grace," Jess added.

Colin groaned. "I guess we don't have much of a choice, do we?" Jess shook her head, an amused smile on her face. Colin stuck out his hand. "Fine. Let's just get through this week."

"Deal," Jess said, shaking his hand.

They walked all the way to Colin's house and when they got there, Colin asked, "Are you coming in?"

Jess laughed shortly and answered, "Shouldn't I be the one asking that?"

"Oh yeah," Colin said. "This is so weird."

"Obviously." Jess looked him up and down and then tilted her head toward the house. "Come on. Cass will probably want to see… you."

"I don't know if I can handle Cass like this."

"You have to," Jess insisted. "We have to act like nothing is wrong until we switch back."

"And if we never do?" Colin asked hesitantly.

Jess bit her bottom lip and shook her head. "I don't know."

Before either Colin or Jess could say any more, the door opened and Cass stared at them in a startled surprise. Jess blushed at being caught with Colin, but Colin merely lifted a brow. Cass gave them both weird looks.

"What are you guys doing?" Cass asked suspiciously.

"Uhh…" Colin said. "We were just…"

"At Dairy Queen," Jess finished.

"Together?" Cass asked in surprise.

"After dancing," Colin added.

"And soccer practice. I went with Ian," Jess said.

Cass' eyes widened and her face went bright red. She grabbed Colin's hand and said, "Come on, Jess. We need to talk."

Colin had no choice but to follow Cass up to her room, while Jess was left to wander into the house, lamenting the fact that that was *her* conversation Colin was having. She sighed and watched them scurry up the stairs.

Cass took Colin into her room, shut the door hard and then turned to him with a giant smile. "Okay, tell me everything."

"Uhh... what?" Colin said unceremoniously.

"Ian," Cass said simply. "What happened? Did he ask about me?"

Colin thought back to the brief conversation he and the girls had shared with Jess and Ian. He remembered the girls telling him that Cass would be so jealous if she knew they were sharing lunch with Ian, but he couldn't remember if Ian had asked about Cass specifically.

"I don't think so," Colin finally answered. "Why?"

Cass' eagerness faded as she slumped down on her bed. "I just thought... he might have asked."

"Because," Colin swallowed past the lump in his throat, "you think he might like you?"

"Do *you* think that?" Cass asked, perking up a bit.

Recalling some of the bits of conversation that Colin had had with Ian, he knew that Ian did, in fact, like Cass. Then again, Ian liked all girls. Colin debated in his head whether he should tell Cass anything, the whole time not wanting to have this conversation at all.

Meanwhile, Cass was reciting a list of reasons why she thought Ian might or might not like her. "And then there was that one time that he told me I looked pretty. Oh, but he also told you he liked your hair that day."

Ian had told both Cass and Jess they looked nice on the same day? Some sort of brotherly protective instinct kicked into Colin's sub-conscious and he asked, "Cass, do you really think Ian is the type of guy you should date?"

"Why not?" Cass asked. "He's cute, athletic, nice…"

Colin hesitated. He wanted to tell Cass that Ian was a player, that he would only date her once and then get bored. But he knew that if he said any of that, Cass would get suspicious as to how *Jess* would know all that. Instead, he tried to come up with a polite way of telling Cass that Ian was a schmuck. But how would Jess put it?

"All of those are fine qualities," Colin said, trying to incorporate a big word he felt Jess would use. "But is that anything to base a relationship on?"

"A relationship?" Cass laughed. "I'm just hoping for a date right now. How could I possibly know if I want a relationship with him if I don't date him?"

"Hmm…" Colin hadn't really thought about that. Was that how girls saw things? Weren't they all just after diamond rings, even at such a young age? "Good point," he conceded.

Cass smiled. "So, do you think he'll ask me?"

Colin forced a titter and answered, "I hope so."

Cass took Colin's hands. "See? This is why you're my best friend. You're just so supportive."

Colin looked down at their hands and out of pure reaction, he squeezed them. He hadn't realized he'd done such a good job at being Jessica until he said something that Cass considered supportive. It made him feel… good. And strange. Too strange. Obviously Jess' body was doing something weird to his emotions.

Cass went to open her bedroom door, and when she did, Jess almost fell right in. It was obvious she'd had her ear to the door, and Colin gave her an amused smile. Cass, on the other hand, was less than amused.

"Colin!" Cass exclaimed, crossing her arms. "Were you listening in on our conversation?" Without waiting for the answer, she just shook her head at him and frowned profusely.

"N-no," Jess stammered. "I was just looking for you."

"What for?" Cass asked.

"I thought maybe…" Jess searched for any appropriate reason why she, as Colin, should have been looking for Cass. "Do you want to go the mall with me?"

"You hate going to the mall," Cass answered.

"Yeah, you definitely do," Colin said with a warning flash in his eyes.

Jess clenched her jaw and then forced a smile at both of them. "Remember all of those times I told you I hated going to the mall? Well, I didn't really mean that. The mall's not so bad."

Colin's eyes bugged out of his head as Cass relaxed her stance. Jess shrugged with a crooked smile. That would teach Colin to not be an idiot anymore.

"You really want to go to the mall with me?" Cass asked sceptically.

"Sure, why not?" Jess answered. Then, shooting Colin a glance, she added, "Just you and me."

Colin's jaw dropped as Cass turned to him. "Do you mind, Jess?"

Colin snapped his mouth shut. "I guess not. I should go home anyway. Mom and Dad probably miss me."

Jess cleared her throat. Was Colin really going to play this game with her? "You know what? On second thought, maybe you should come."

"No, that's alright. You two need bonding time," Colin said with a wink.

Cass looked back and forth between Colin and Jess, her eyebrows drawn in. "Is there something going on between you two?"

"No!" Colin said.

"Ew, no way," Jess conceded.

Cass shook her head. "Okay, whatever. Listen, I'll see you later, okay Jess?"

As Cass hugged Colin goodbye, Colin asked, "Later?"

"Yeah, for the movie, remember? Mom and I will pick you up at seven," Cass reminded him. Or rather, she informed him, since this was the first time he was hearing about it.

"Oh, I – I forgot." Colin reached for the front door handle, dreading what kind of movie Jess and Cass had picked out. "I can't. I'm sorry. I have, like, a thing." Jess started furiously shaking her head as Colin floundered around for a plausible excuse for not going. "A family thing."

Jess rolled her eyes and Cass obviously tried to conceal her disappointment. "That's okay," Cass said. "We can rent a movie next week or something."

"Sure," Colin found himself saying. "See you later, girls."

Jess crossed her arms and gave him a warning look. "Not funny, *Jess.*"

"I mean… Cass, Colin… Jacobs siblings." Colin left the house quickly, hoping Cass wouldn't think twice about his slip of the tongue.

Jess was elated to finally be having some fun, especially since it meant she would get to spend more time with Cass. Of course, it wasn't exactly the most favourable of situations, but it would have to do.

SIX

When Cass and Jess informed Mrs. Jacobs that they needed a ride to the mall, the older woman raised an eyebrow at them, one hand placed on her hip. She looked back and forth between them in silence.

"So, what did you do to get him to agree to go with you?" she finally asked, directing her question at Cass.

Cass shrugged. "He just offered, so of course I couldn't say no."

Cass and her mother shared a giggle as Jess looked on, the corners of her mouth tilting up in an amused smile.

"Alright kids, I'll drop you off," Mrs. Jacobs said, reaching for her keys off the key rack by the front door. "But you'll have to take the bus back."

"That's fine," Jess said quickly. She was just anxious to get to the mall and do something more fun than playing soccer and not having milkshakes.

"Nice to have you in such an agreeable mood," Mrs. Jacobs said.

"Yeah, you should be like this more often," Cass said.

"You're right," Jess said, knowing full well that she was ruining Colin's tough-guy rep. "I should. Maybe I will be from now on."

Cass and Mrs. Jacobs looked at each other wide-eyed then they both laughed again. Mrs. Jacobs shook her head as she left the house, Cass trailing behind her with an equally disbelieving shake of the head. Jess tried to stifle a laugh. Colin would hate her for making him look so vulnerable.

Jess and Cass wandered the mall in an almost comfortable silence, passively choosing not to go into any stores. Cass would have preferred looking around at some clothing or maybe some of the blingy jewellery stores. But she figured Colin would hate looking at those things, and there was no way she was going to pick out Xbox games with him.

Of course, Jess would have given anything to go to the same stores Cass wanted to see. But she knew it would tip Cass off if *Colin* were suddenly interested in woman's clothing. Not only that, but it would be extremely awkward if Cass thought Colin was trying to cross-dress or something.

Then Jess had an idea. She remembered one time when she and Cass had gone into a Le Château and out of sheer boredom, they'd gone into the men's section and ooed and ahhed over the fancy suits. After that, every once in a while, they'd go to the guy's section of a store just to fantasize over how good some of the clothing would look on guys.

Jess stopped at the next store they passed by and pointed toward it. "Want to go in?"

It was a store that had clothing for girls and guys and at first Cass didn't know whether Jess was serious or not. "You… want to go in there? Why?"

"Look at me, Cass," Jess said, gesturing down at herself. "I think we can both agree that I have no fashion sense."

Cass giggled as she scrutinized Colin's clothing. Jess had tried not to make Colin look like a slob earlier when she was dressing his body, but it was hard when Colin really *didn't* have any fashion sense.

"So, what? You want to buy some new clothes?" Cass asked.

"Sure." Jess shrugged. "You can…help me."

Cass shook her head with a slight smile. "Alright. This is weird, but a good weird I guess."

Cass and Jess entered the store, and the first thing Jess saw was a cute blue summer dress with pink flowers all over it. She couldn't help it – she blurted out, "That would look so good on you!"

49

Cass glanced at the dress briefly. "Yeah, it kind of would," she said in a surprised voice. "But we're not here for me, so don't think you can get out of trying on a million things here."

Jess faked an eye roll and a groan, but secretly, she was excited. Not only did she love buying clothes, but now she actually got to a dress a real boy. How nice of Colin to lend her his body so he could be her Ken doll.

She dismissed that last thought from her head, deeming it altogether too creepy to dwell on. She tried to convince herself that the only reason she was buying Colin new clothes was because she didn't want to look like a slob, no matter whose body she was inhabiting.

While Jess was dispelling so-called creepy thoughts from her mind, Cass was already busy pulling shirts, shorts, and pants from racks. Jess knew Cass' routine well. Cass touched every piece of fabric to make sure it "felt right," and if that was sufficient, she'd pull the article of clothing off the rack to look at it. And if it looked right, she'd keep it on her arm and move on. Once her arm got full, she'd ask someone to open up a room for her, and then add a few more pieces to the pile before trying them on. Of course, Jess would be trying them on this time.

Not that she'd ever admit it, but Jess had a fabulous time trying on clothes, even in Colin's body. Or maybe especially since she was in his body. Creepy again, yes, but still kind of… fun.

Cass took her to a few more stores that she said would have great clothes just for Colin's body type. There was one in particular that Cass *insisted* Colin should buy something from. Jess already knew the store she was talking about, because it was one that she and Cass had gushed over many times before. It had never occurred to her that it would be just the store for Colin, but now that Cass mentioned it, Jess had to agree.

It was only after they'd been to about five stores and Jess had an armful of shopping bags that she realized she'd used her own money for Colin's new wardrobe. She doubted Colin would pay her back or ever give her anything in return for any of it. It was another thought that she knew she should just let go. Because she knew that if she and

Colin didn't switch back, this would be the body she'd have to dress… forever.

"So, why the sudden transformation?" Cass asked, disrupting Jess' inner thoughts.

"I guess I just wanted a change," Jess said, with more truth than Cass would ever realize. "I think I'm all shopped out for the day, though."

"That's alright," Cass said with a smirk. "I'm surprised you even lasted that long. Just one more thing, Col."

"What's that?"

"You're going to need a new haircut for all those clothes," Cass said, flicking a lock of hair off Jess' forehead with her forefinger.

Jess bit her lip. Colin's hair was a mess. It fell past his ears, down past his eyebrows and was generally unkempt. But would Colin hate her if she got his hair cut for him? Would he hate it if she made him look nice? As nice as he could look, that is. She'd already spent a lot of money today. Then she remembered that she was stuck in his body. And his shaggy hair.

"You know what?" Jess said thoughtfully. "Let's do it."

"Yay!" Cass said, clapping her hands. "This has been the most exciting shopping trip I've ever been on with you. I can't wait to tell Jess all about it."

"Oh, you're not really going to tell her, are you?" Jess asked, cringing honestly. She was fairly certain that Colin would not want all the nitty gritty details of how Jess had bought him a ton of clothes and a new haircut.

"Yes, of course," Cass answered, steering Jess toward a fancy beauty salon. "I tell her everything. Hi, Mary." She smiled at the receptionist.

"Hey, Cass," the receptionist answered with a smile of her own.

She had a stud in her nose and half of her hair was pink while the other half was blue. Cass and Jess both knew Mary well, since this was their salon of choice, and Jess tried hard not to look like she recognized her.

"Who's this handsome man?" she asked. "Your new BF?

Cass laughed out loud and Jess scowled with a slight blush. "No," Cass said when she caught her breath. "This is my brother. And as you can see, he desperately needs a new style." Cass fingered Colin's hair as she spoke.

"Ohhh," Mary cooed. "I see. Emergency cut!" she called to the back.

Feminine laughter spilled out to the front counter. Three women of varying ages and hair styles all came forward and started touching Jess' head, discussing what should be done to it. Jess managed to look suitably uncomfortable, which wasn't far from the truth. Two of the women went back to their own clients and the third led Jess to a chair.

Jess wasn't allowed to watch as the woman cut Colin's hair, but she knew from experience that a lot was getting cut off and that it would be fantastic once she was done. As per usual, this hairdresser had a way of getting Jess to talk about everything. Jess had to concentrate very hard on saying the right things and not giving away who she really was. So she stuck to soccer practice and how there were try-outs, and even threw in an "I hope I get first string!"

But when the shopping spree was over, Jess remembered that she was just acting a part. She may have been the one to buy all those clothes, but it was *Colin* that everyone would see wearing them. It was Colin with a nice new haircut. It was Colin who was hoping for first string. And Jess didn't know how long she'd be able to handle that before what and who she really was would come to the surface. She couldn't pretend to be a boy forever.

When they were on the bus back home, Jess asked Cass a question she'd had on her mind for a long time, almost as long as she'd known Cass. "What happened to us?" she asked timidly, not knowing what Cass' response might be.

"What do you mean?" Cass asked back, furrowing her eyebrows.

"I mean… we used to be good friends," Jess stated. "What changed?"

Cass shrugged and looked away, trying not to let Jess know how much the question affected her. "We're into different stuff, I guess."

Jess nodded. It wasn't exactly an acceptable excuse, but then she didn't know what went on between Cass and Colin when she wasn't near them.

"You're a good singer," Jess said after a few more minutes of silence.

Cass rolled her eyes. "You always tell me I'm awful," she said, with a touch of hurt in her voice.

"You're not," Jess said. "Those vocal exercises, though…"

"Oh, Colin," Cass whined, hitting her on the arm. "I already told you why it's so important for me to do those every day."

Cass had actually never told Jess about the exercises, but even though she was curious, she didn't ask. Instead she said softly, "I know. But… you could just sing around the house once in a while. That's good for you too, right?"

"Thanks for the tip, Maestro," Cass said sarcastically. But at least she'd softened her tone of voice a bit.

The whole time Jess and Cass were at the mall, Colin moped around Jess' room. He had nothing else to do. He didn't know what Jess would have been doing if she were here instead of him. He, on the other hand, wanted nothing more than to go out and kick a soccer ball around. But he couldn't do that because it would look really weird, and also Jess had no appropriate clothing for that kind of activity.

Since Colin was stuck in Jess' body and her room, he took the liberty of looking through all of her stuff. His momentary twinge of guilt at the idea was quickly diminished by the fact that Jess had probably done the same in his room.

He'd already looked through all her clothes that morning. A second brief glance at her closet confirmed what he knew: that he would never dress like her if he were a girl. Which, unfortunately and for the time being, he was. But only for a while. He hadn't yet given up on the hope that he and Jess would switch back.

The top of Jess' dresser was full of little girly trinkets that were obviously all gifts at one point or another. Girls never bought stuff like that for themselves and they only ever kept them because they were a gift from someone meaningful. He knew that from the rare glances he stole inside Cass' bedroom. He knew it, because she still had the ceramic pony that Colin himself had painted for her when he was ten. Art didn't really appeal to him anymore, but at the time Cass had thought it was the greatest gift ever.

Jess' desk was a little neater than the dresser. Colin opened the drawers, but inside was mostly boring stuff: a stapler, pens, excessive amounts of lined paper, sticky notes, and paper clips. On top of the desk was Jess' laptop, which was surprisingly silver-encased instead of pink. Next to the laptop was an iPod in its dock and a series of different coloured sticky notes.

Colin left the iPod alone, knowing full well Jess' tastes in music would be vastly different from his own. Instead, he read some of the sticky notes. "Recital this Friday!!!" "Practice the pas de bourrée." "Get Cass a date." "Get ME a date."

Colin backed up one. Get Cass a date? Why would Jess be getting Cass a date? Couldn't Cass do that all on her own? And more importantly, did Jess now expect him to "get Cass a date" since he was pretending to be her? Well it didn't matter if Jess did want him to; there was no way he would. Cass was still his little sister, no matter whose body he was in. She was too young for dating anyway. Especially if dating involved Ian. Which it wouldn't, if Colin had anything to say about it.

Finally when Colin couldn't handle the solitude anymore, he texted Jess, "Let's meet after dinner."

"So soon?" she texted back a few minutes later.

"Yes. We need to be ready."

"Shouldn't we at least wait until it's dark?"

"As soon as everyone's asleep then."

"Fine. My place or yours?"

"I thought you'd never ask."

"Don't be a pig, Colin."

"Mine… or, yours really. You have a big backyard."

It was true. The Lewises had a huge backyard that backed onto a forest. If they went out there, no one would notice, and they would be able to practice freely.

"Fine. I'll see how early I can get away."

Colin sighed. What, like Jess had huge plans that night in *his* body? How long would it take her to get to her house?

Colin had to content himself with what he had. He ate dinner with Jess' parents, who were quite reserved and rarely spoke at the table. That was fine with him, since he wouldn't know what to say to them. And after that, while he waited for Jess to show up, he played around on her computer, trying hard not to snoop too much.

Finally, Colin heard a ping on Jess' window. He looked out into the dark and didn't see anyone. But then another pebble hit the window and he knew Jess had arrived. He rushed down the stairs and out the back door as quietly as he could so that he wouldn't alert Jess' parents. When he got outside, he came face-to-face with...

Well, it sort of looked like him, except that now his hair looked like it came out of a magazine. And the clothes Jess had put on him! The jeans were too tight and the collared shirt made him look like a nerd. His eyes flashed as he came toward her.

"What did you do?!" Colin exclaimed as quietly as he could possibly manage. It came out as a startled whisper-yell.

"O-oh," Jess stammered, touching her hair. "This?"

"Yes, *that*," Colin said. Then he pointed to the shirt. "And that, and those jeans. Those aren't mine."

"No, but they look really good on you, don't you think?" Jess asked, her nervousness making Colin's voice sound almost meek.

"No, they look awful," Colin countered.

Jess looked down at the ground, embarrassed at his response and that she'd gone through the trouble to make him look good. Without another word, she started to walk away toward the gate.

"Wait," Colin called her back, grabbing out to stop her from leaving. He wrapped Jess' tiny hand around his own seemingly much larger forearm. "Why did you do all that?" he asked when she stopped.

"Because…" She sighed. "Because you always look like a slob."

"Gee, thanks."

"But you obviously have the potential to look nice," she added. "I mean… you *do* look good like this," she said sincerely.

"Well… now I don't know whether to feel insulted or complimented," Colin said, letting go of Jess' arm.

"It's true, okay? Plus, Cass really liked picking out clothes with… with *you*," Jess informed him.

Colin didn't know what to say, so he didn't say anything. That whole time Cass thought he was enjoying buying clothes and getting a haircut, and he'd had no part of it. To his surprise, a surge of jealousy rushed through him. He tried to put it from his mind, but he couldn't help asking himself *why* he was jealous.

"Let's just practice some stuff tonight and move on," Jess suggested. Their conversation was getting them nowhere and she didn't want to explain to Colin that she was afraid of being stuck in his body and that was the biggest reason she'd made all those changes to his appearance.

"Fine. Soccer first."

Jess shook her head. "Dancing. It takes a lot more time to perfect."

Colin groaned, but instead of arguing, he asked, "It's always going to be like this between us, isn't it?"

Jess smirked. "Probably."

SEVEN

"Lines, Colin. Lines," Jess repeated for the tenth time in the last five minutes.

Colin sighed and dropped his arms. They'd been practising dancing for the last forty-five minutes – no, the last hour. Jess had been "instructing" him on technique and lecturing him about his forms. And every time she did, he would whine about how he didn't actually know how to dance and that Jess would have to go down to the basics.

"Jess, I told you a million times," Colin started. "These are the best lines I've got!"

Jess stared at Colin and after what seemed like an eternity, she gave a slight shake of her head. "I can't believe you're making me do this, but clearly I have no choice."

"What are you talking about?" Colin asked testily.

"You need to extend your arm to the fullest," she explained, stretching out her right arm at a forty-five degree angle, her fingers stretched out like a fan. She then brought her left arm up in a graceful sweep to be level with the other arm. When they were both in position, Jess raised them both up above her head, reaching toward the now-high moon, and tilted her head up to look.

Colin watched as Jess took off her shoes and then raised herself on her toes. Without speaking, she spun one of her legs out with the other one following, turning her arms around her as she completed the graceful spin. She finished the spin with a tasteful plié after which Colin applauded her. Jess flashed him a smile.

"I had no idea I could do that!" Colin exclaimed.

"You *didn't* do it," Jess countered, her smiling fading. "I did. Although I have to admit I didn't think your body would actually be able to handle all that."

"I know. It is a pretty awesome body, isn't it?" he smirked.

"My point is," she ignored his comment, "my body knows exactly how to do those moves."

"Then why isn't it working?" he asked.

"Because you don't want to do it," she answered. "You're resisting, so it's all coming out wrong."

"Maybe I'm just a bad dancer," he suggested.

"Clearly you're not," Jess said with a bow and wink. Colin just shook his head. "Trust me, Col, you can do this. I'll show you."

Jess came to stand behind Colin and without giving him a chance to retaliate, she took a firm grip of his hand. Though Colin groaned, he didn't pull away as Jess forced his arm up and over his head in what was supposed to be a natural movement. Colin pulled his arm back and grimaced.

"Why'd you stop? That was looking so much better," Jess commented.

"How could something that uncomfortable look good in any way?" Colin whined.

"You get used to it."

Without waiting, Jess lifted Colin's arm up again and then guided him through the rest of the steps. There was a series of slow, graceful arm movements before the spin. Colin managed to get the arm arcs just right, but the spin was a mess. Jess pointed out every part of Colin's body that he had to use for it and how he had to use them, and then made him do the spin really slowly.

"There, good," Jess said soothingly. "Now you try it on your own."

"Okay," Colin said hesitantly.

Colin started with the preceding step and then moved into the spin much more naturally than Jess thought he would have. Colin turned twice, moving his arms and legs in just the right places. But just as he went to end his spin, he miss-stepped and tripped. Jess threw out her arms to try to catch him but instead ended up falling with him.

"Oof!"

"Umm, sorry."

"That wasn't part of the spin."

"I know… thanks for catching my fall, though."

"Anytime. Now get off me."

Colin jumped up quickly, embarrassed that he'd fallen right into Jess' arms. His own arms. And worse than that was the fact that he kind of liked the way Jess had caught him while he was falling. He cleared those thoughts from his mind as he leaned a hand down to help Jess up.

"Sorry if I got your new clothes all dirty," Colin said, still feeling awkward.

"It's fine," Jess said, brushing the back of her off. "Maybe we should try soccer now."

Colin sighed in relief. "Oh good. I was starting to get worried I'd never be good at anything again."

Jess chuckled. "You weren't that bad. I, on the other hand, have no idea how soccer works. At all."

"Thanks." Colin paused. "Okay, anyway… Soccer. So we have the midfielders, the defenders, the forwards and the goalkeeper. We'll worry about the goalkeeper later; he's not as important to you right now. Now, the defenders are there…well to defend, obviously. You've got your full-back, your wing-back, your centre-back and your sweepers. Now, sweepers are really just –"

"Colin," Jess cut off his ramblings and placed her hand on his shoulder. "What are you doing?"

"I'm explaining the positions to you," Colin said like this should have been obvious to her.

"But why do I need to know all of that?" Jess asked.

Colin's beautifully plucked eyebrows drew together furiously. "How else are you supposed to understand how soccer works unless you know what everyone's doing on the field?"

"Colin. I don't even know how to kick a soccer ball properly," Jess informed him. "Not to mention that I don't even know what position you play."

Colin burst out laughing while Jess just stared at him. "Well, that must have made practice pretty awkward this morning, eh?"

"You could say that," she muttered. "Your coach got so annoyed that he benched me."

That comment snapped Colin out of his mirth. "What?" he exclaimed. "No. No, no, no. This is so much worse than I thought." Colin put his face in his hands and continued mumbling negativities.

Jess watched him for a few minutes, allowing him his private pity party until she had had enough. "Okay, okay," she said taking his hands. "It's not the end of the world. That's why I'm still out here, right? To make things okay."

"Okay. I know," Colin said, giving her a weak smile. "I'm just so... so... emotional."

Jess nodded sagely. "It comes with the territory. Now back up a bit. Tell me what your position is."

"I'm a centre mid-fielder," Colin said.

"Which means?"

"I'm a liaison between defence and attack. Not only do midfielders have to try to stop people from getting to the actual defence, but they're also responsible for getting the ball up to the attackers." Colin watched Jess chew her lip and added, "It's kind of a big deal. Especially for a centre, because you have a lot of control... Jess?"

"I don't know if I can do this," Jess said quietly.

"Jess," Colin said firmly, "if I can do a perfect spin for you, right now, will you at least be willing to learn?"

Jess looked down at her shoes for a few moments and then finally said, "Fine."

Colin took his position, did a leading step and then turned gracefully, ending this time in the right spot.

"Well," Jess said, "the ending was a bit messy, but at least you didn't fall this time."

Colin smiled. "Let me go grab that soccer ball and I'll show you a proper kick."

Jess sighed. She knew she'd have to do this for Colin. He'd just spent an hour learning how to do some of the routine for her recital; the least she could do was kick a ball around for a few minutes.

When Colin returned, he said, "The first thing you should know is that you don't kick the ball with your toes. You have to actually point your toes down – you already know how to do that, though, right? – and then hit the ball with the top of your foot."

He lightly kicked the ball to Jess, who kicked it weakly back. Colin tried again, and this time, Jess' kick was more confident.

"There, that's it," Colin complimented.

After they had kicked the ball back and forth for a few minutes, Jess asked, "What position does Ian play?"

"Wasn't it obvious at practice?" Colin asked in confusion.

"I was sort of in a daze," Jess confessed.

"Right. He's a centre forward."

"And he…?"

"Scores all the goals and gets all the glory," Colin finished for her.

Jess laughed. "Not that you're bitter or anything."

"I'm not," Colin said plainly. "But what I said was true. Centre forwards have one job, and that is to score goals. And naturally, anyone who scores goals gets all the attention."

"I see," Jess said, still trying to determine whether or not Colin really was a little jealous of his friend. "So he's kind of like David Beckham."

"Um, no," Colin said. "David Beckham is a right midfielder."

"So?"

"So, he's not a forward."

"But he's all famous and stuff," Jess said.

"Yeah, but a right midfielder's main job isn't just to score goals," Colin explained. "Not like a centre forward. If you're going to go for an analogy like that, you'd have to say Ian is more like Sidney Crosby."

"But… that's hockey, isn't it?" Jess asked.

"Ah, you do know something about sports," Colin said, raising an eyebrow. "Yes, that's hockey. But literally, all Sidney Crosby does is score goals. He has no other job."

"But he's good at it."

"He's very good at it, yes."

"Is Ian good?" Jess asked.

"Yes," Colin answered without a trace of contempt in his voice.

"And that doesn't bother you?" Jess asked as she kicked the ball wide of Colin.

He walked over and picked the ball up, wedging it between his arm and his hip. "Why should it?"

"Because he gets all the glory," Jess pointed out. "You said it yourself.

"Oh." Colin said. "That part kind of bugs me, since he's so arrogant. But to be honest, I'm just as good, if not a better soccer player than he is. And I like my position. I wouldn't trade that."

Jess nodded. "He never really seemed arrogant to me."

"You'll see," Colin said softly.

"I don't understand," Jess said. "Isn't Ian your friend? Why do you put him down?"

Colin laughed shortly. "I'm not putting him down, Jess. Ian knows I think he's arrogant sometimes, and Ian has no problem telling me I'm a sore loser. That doesn't exactly make us enemies."

"Well, that seems like... a healthy relationship," Jess said uncertainly. "I guess."

"It's not the same for guys as it is for girls," Colin said. "Girls will be best of friends to each others' faces, but then talk about each other behind their backs. Guys are just upfront about all that crap from the start."

"Well, you just have us pegged, don't you?" Jess asked in an annoyed tone of voice.

"Yeah, pretty much."

"Right, well, I think that's enough practice for tonight," Jess said, starting to walk toward the back door of the house.

"Wait," Colin called her back.

"What?" Jess asked, spinning back around.

"Well for one thing, this is my house," Colin said, a teasing light in his eyes.

"Oh yeah."

"And for another thing, we've barely touched the basics of soccer," he pointed out.

"I know, but it's late," she said. "I promise, we'll do more of the soccer stuff next time."

"Okay, but we really should work hard on this, you know?"

"Yes, I'm well aware of what's at stake," Jess snapped.

"It's just that –" Colin cut his sentence short.

"That what?" Jess asked.

"Nothing. Goodnight, Jess."

Colin watched Jess walk back to the gate before entering the house again. He had been about to tell her that making first string this year meant a lot to him, and that it was so, *so* important that she play well to make that happen. He had almost confessed to her that if she failed to do that for him, he'd have to suffer through watching Ian get all the glory and Colin wouldn't even be there to say that he was part of the same team.

But he had decided not to tell any of that to Jess. She would insist that he really was jealous of Ian, and that he was being selfish for pushing her so hard to do well. A part of him knew that it was selfish to want her to do well, because essentially she'd be doing his job for him. On the other hand, he didn't exactly take her dancing seriously. Maybe if he did, she'd take his soccer playing seriously. It was worth a thought anyway.

EIGHT

Sunday morning dawned fresh and bright, along with a pounding sound at Colin's door. Jess woke with a start and checked the clock: 9 a.m. Why was she being woken up so early? This was supposed to be her sleep-in day.

"Colin!" It was Mr. Jacobs, his voice being muffled by the door. "No more late Jacobs stuff. We're getting a reputation at church."

Laughter trailed away down the hall as Jess dragged a hand down her face. Church? Jess didn't do church. And she forgot that the Jacobs family did. Colin hadn't mentioned it, although she supposed she should have known. Cass had offered to take her enough times for Jess to know it was a big deal to them.

Jess dragged herself out of bed, getting ready as quickly as she could. She actually had no idea when church started and she didn't want to contribute to the Jacobses' "reputation." At least she'd have another chance to dress Colin in something nice. That was one thing she knew about church – everyone dressed pretty.

When Jess looked at herself in the mirror – or rather, at Colin's face – she wondered whether or not he was shaving yet. There was a fine layer of peach fuzz, but Jess decided it wasn't worth it to try to shave. Then it occurred to her that her legs, the legs Colin currently possessed, were never going to be shaved as long as Colin was in them.

In the kitchen, everyone was already finishing up breakfast; "Mom" wiping her mouth meticulously, "Dad" slurping up the last of his coffee, and Cass taking the last bite of her eggs.

"Colin, finally," Mrs. Jacobs said. She held an egg sandwich out to him. "Here, you'll have to eat in the car. Let's go, everyone."

On the drive over to the church, Jess sat very still and silent as the others talked. She wasn't even listening to them. She had never been to a church service before, not even for Christmas or Easter, and she didn't really know what to expect. And the longer the drive got, the more nervous she started to feel about it.

Finally, they reached the church, its tall steeple practically glowing in the sunlight. Jess surreptitiously looked the church up and down. The building looked new, but it was an old-fashioned style, with arches above the double doorways, and a bell tower just below the giant white cross. The large grey bricks made it look like it could have come out of the Middle Ages, except that the bricks were all equal in size and didn't look like they were hundreds of years old.

The parking lot had only a few cars in it, and Jess wondered why so few people needed such a large building. Cass got out of the car and hurried to the side-door entrance, while Mr. and Mrs. Jacobs went to retrieve two Saran Wrap covered platters from the back of the van. Jess trailed behind them into the church because she didn't know what else there was to do.

The large foyer inside had a much more modern look than the outside of the building. Off to the right was an information table where a little old lady was setting out some brochures, books, and envelopes. Next to her was a hallway that led to some other recess of the church, and glass doors with signs that said NURSERY, SUNDAY SCHOOL, and SUPPLIES.

To the left were two sets of glass double doors. Wanting to get a closer look at what was inside, Jess inched over to the glass and glanced inside. She caught a glimpse of what looked like a band forming onstage. Cass was just about to pick up a microphone when Mrs. Jacobs called, "Colin, don't bug your sister."

Jess pulled herself back. It made sense now. Cass was singing for the church and so they must have arrived early for her to warm up, which was why no one else was here now. She wanted to go inside the large room with all the stretched out seats, but Colin's mom had already reprimanded her.

"Colin," an old-sounding voice called from behind her. Jess turned around. It was the lady at the info desk. "Would you be a dear and get that box down for me?" she asked in a frail voice, pointing to a box on a shelf way above her head.

"Sure," Jess said. She went quickly over to the shelf and pulled the heavy box down with ease.

"Oh, Colin, you're a sweetheart. Here," the lady scrounged around in her purse and pulled out a Ziploc full of Scotch Mints. "Take one," she offered, opening the bag to Jess.

Jess wasn't particularly in the mood for old-lady candy, but she didn't want to offend anyone, especially not in a church. So she took one and said, "Thanks."

"I like your new haircut," the lady said. "Is that for your girlfriend?"

Jess blushed and said, "No, I don't have a girlfriend. Cass helped me with it." The old lady nodded slowly.

"My granddaughter is coming to town next weekend," the lady continued on, giving Jess a warm smile. "I know how well you two get along."

Jess chuckled nervously. She tried edging away to end the conversation as she said, "Well, I can't wait to see her again."

"Ooh, she'll be so thrilled to see you!" the woman practically squealed, clasping her hands together.

"Right," Jess said, attempting a friendly smile. "I have to go… help my mom. I'll… see you."

"Not until you give me a hug, young man," the woman said, wagging a finger at her. "I'm surprised I haven't gotten one, yet."

"Oh. Sorry." Jess leaned forward and down to give the little woman a loose hug.

"There, that's better. Now, go on."

Jess walked toward the hallway as the old woman started humming off-key, opening the box Jess had pulled down for her. Jess shook her head. Apparently this church doubled as a match-making service. The best she could do was pray that she and Colin switched back before next Sunday, which seemed appropriate considering the building she was roaming.

As Jess walked down the hall, she was grateful that there were signs posted around, directing her to various rooms of the church. The kitchen sign with the arrow was particularly helpful, since she figured that's where Colin's mom and dad had likely gone with those food platters.

She stepped into the kitchen where Mrs. Jacobs and three other ladies were standing around, unwrapping plates of food and setting cookies out on trays. They were all laughing at something one of them had said, but they quieted down when Jess walked in.

"No snacking before church, Colin," Lady #1 said. She looked a little like Dolly Parton, only with much less hair.

"You know the rules," Lady #2 said. She shook a finger at him and then went back to arranging cold cuts.

"I –" Jess was cut off.

"Oh, one little cookie couldn't hurt," Lady #3, an older model of the other two, said, holding out a cookie in Jess' direction.

"What's up, son?" Mrs. Jacobs asked kindly, scrutinizing Jess with a worried look.

"Nothing, Mom," Jess said hastily, glad to finally get a word in. She ignored the proffered cookie and stepped deeper into the kitchen. "I was just wondering if you needed any help."

Ladies #1 and #2 cackled in what Jess guessed was supposed to be a teasing way. She ignored their laughter and kept her eyes fixed on Mrs. Jacobs who was now smiling.

"No, honey, that's alright," she said. "Why don't you go find your father outside?"

"Sure…" Jess said uncertainly. She left the kitchen while the ladies stared back at her in silence. Now which way to the outside?

Jess roamed around for another five minutes, looking for signs, getting lost in the hallways, apologizing for walking in on a Sunday school class and then finally, *finally* finding her way to the back door. When she stepped outside, she saw Colin's dad standing with two other men. Mr. Jacobs caught her eye and, without breaking the conversation, nodded his head in indication that Jess should come over.

Jess listened to the men finish their conversation, after which Mr. Jacobs took her by the shoulder and pushed her slightly toward one of the men. "Colin, this is Ed Stern. He just moved to town with his family. This is my son, Colin," he said with a hint of pride in his voice.

Ed put out his hand by way of greeting, and Jess took it in what she hoped was a firm handshake.

"Nice to meet you, Mr. Stern," Jess said.

"Likewise, Colin," Ed said.

"I was just telling Ed and Clint here," Mr. Jacobs indicated the younger man standing with them, "about your soccer playing. Ed has a son about your age, who might be interested. What do you think?"

Jess didn't know what to say. She could barely play soccer herself and after that horrible practice yesterday, she doubted the coach would take her advice on letting in another team member. She decided on a safe answer.

"Soccer try-outs are this Friday," she told Ed. "If he's good, I don't see why he shouldn't come out."

"See?" Mr. Jacobs said. "I told you Colin would say that."

Jess breathed a secret sigh of relief for having done well at playing Colin as Ed nodded slowly. "Well, I'll have to tell him. He's really into soccer."

"So am I," Jess said, surprising herself at the enthusiasm with which she announced Colin's passion. "I mean… it's just such a great sport, right?"

Clint smiled and finally spoke up. "You never change, Colin."

Jess smiled back, pleased with her performance. She followed the men back into the church that was finally starting to fill up. People greeted Jess and Colin's parents with handshakes, hugs, smiles, and little inside jokes that Jess knew she would never get.

Though Jess would never admit it, she kind of liked the way everyone said hi to her, asked how she was, and took the time to have little conversations with her. Even if it was really Colin they were greeting, it still made her feel all warm and fuzzy inside. It also made her wonder what Colin had done to gain such great favour with the church folks.

Colin's parents ushered Jess into what she assumed was their regular pew. Jess had the great fortune of being squished between Mrs. Jacobs and an older man who smelled vaguely of wood smoke. As soon as she sat down and started to get comfy, a man at the front of the room spoke into the microphone he was holding and asked everyone to remain standing. Jess stood up abruptly, looking around to see if anyone had noticed.

Some lively music started up and people started clapping and saying "Hallelujah!" all around Jess. Cass and four other people on the stage started singing into their mics and the rest of the congregation joined in. There were words displayed on two big screens, but Jess didn't know the songs and she couldn't sing anyway. The best she could do was try to clap along, but even that was difficult since no one else could seem to agree on which beat to clap.

Jess listened for Cass' voice, which came out surprisingly clear. She smiled. Hearing Cass' natural beautiful voice was a nice break from the vocal exercises that Jess was unfortunately starting to get used to. And even though Cass was singing a churchy song that Jess didn't know, Jess could still appreciate the quality of the music.

The worship service finished right when Jess thought that maybe she could get into it. She slumped down gratefully into her seat and made an impossibly small space so Cass could sit with her family. Then some man in a fancy suit came and started lecturing everyone, holding up a faded, leather-bound Bible every once in a while to emphasize his point.

Jess wasn't sure what Colin was like at a church service. She didn't want to let on that she'd never been to one in her life, but on the other hand, she didn't want to make it seem like Colin was really eager to learn or something. So instead, she half-listened to the sermon, making sure to keep her eyes focused on the preacher, but didn't turn to any of the scriptures he pointed out because she wouldn't know where to look anyway.

Throughout the entire experience, Jess kept thinking to herself how she wished she could tell Cass about what she thought of church now that she had finally been. But she knew she couldn't, not even if and when she got back into her own body. The only other option was to discuss it with Colin, but she felt like it was too personal to talk about with her best friend's brother.

Then again, she *was* in his body after all. It didn't really get much more personal than that. She had a strange feeling she'd have to confess to Colin everything that had happened that morning anyway. He probably would have wanted to know that she had made him look good in front of the old lady and the new guy, and that she thought she had acted appropriately for the setting.

Yes, she would tell him about it.

NINE

Colin woke at the crack of noon, stretching leisurely underneath Jess' fluffy comforter and bed sheets. He turned onto his side and squinted at the clock. When he saw that it was already after twelve, he bolted upright in bed, wondering why no one had woken him for church. As soon as he climbed out of the bed, he remembered why: he was still in Jess' body. And presumably, Jess and her family didn't go to church.

Without bothering to dress properly, Colin went down to the kitchen. Mr. Lewis was sitting at the table sipping coffee and reading a Sunday newspaper. Mrs. Lewis was reading a magazine and dipping her fork into some scrambled eggs. When Colin walked in, they both looked up from their reading.

"Well, you're up early," Mr. Lewis commented with raised eyebrows.

"I am?" Colin asked in surprise. How late did Jess get up on Sundays?

Mrs. Lewis merely laughed and asked, "Would you like me to make you some eggs, honey?"

"Sure, I'd like that a lot," Colin said, sitting down at the table.

Without saying a word, Mr. Lewis pulled the comics section out of his newspaper and slid it across the table to Colin. The movement was rhythmically routine. Colin looked down at the comics, a rare gift in his eyes. They never got the paper at home, nor would they have ever taken the time to enjoy it on a Sunday morning. A moment later, Mrs. Lewis came over and set down a plate of eggs with toast in front of Colin, and then quietly went back to her magazine.

Colin started digging into the eggs and then slowed down so that the Lewises wouldn't think their daughter had suddenly been taken over by a barbarian. Or a slob, even if it were true. So Colin took his time eating breakfast – lunch – while he read the comics.

Lunch with the Lewises was, for lack of a better word, nice. That was all Colin could think. It was nice but… different. Quiet. Maybe even a little empty. Colin probably felt this way because he was so used to his mother's chattiness, his father's endless tales, and Cass' constant singing and humming.

Suddenly, Colin felt home-sick. He missed his mom's wonderful Sunday morning breakfasts, no matter how rushed they were at times. He missed his father's wisdom. He even missed Cass' singing and the worship band's music at church. Everything he knew Jess had enjoyed that morning while Colin was asleep. He wished he had awoken earlier so that maybe he could have gone to church.

His appetite lost, he pushed his plate away. Jess' parents didn't really seem to notice. They just kept on reading. Colin handed the comics back to Mr. Lewis and rose from the table. He just needed to get out of the house, away from a life that wasn't his.

"Do you want a ride, Jessica?" Mrs. Lewis asked, lowering her magazine.

Colin turned back around. "A ride?" he asked in confusion.

"To the park?" Mrs. Lewis raised an eyebrow. "Didn't you say you were meeting your friends today?"

"Oh… umm," Colin hesitated. Now he had to hang out with Jess' friends, too? "Yeah, of course." He smiled perkily like he imagined Jess would have at the thought of spending time with her friends. "I wouldn't mind a ride, thanks."

"Okay, whenever you're ready." Mrs. Lewis went back to her magazine.

Colin went back up to Jess' room. On top of missing his family, he would now have to spend time with Jess' girly friends. And be girly himself. He wasn't sure if he was really up to that challenge. Dance class was one thing; that was part of an exchange. But being buddies with her friends? That was entirely different.

With a sigh, Colin opened Jess' closet again. "What exactly does one wear to the park to meet the girls?" Colin blushed slightly at the thought of talking out loud to himself and he checked outside the door to see if anyone was listening. But of course, Mr. and Mrs. Lewis were still downstairs.

"Wow… okay," Colin said to himself. "Why do I suddenly sound like the script for *Sex and the City*?" He shook his head as he surveyed Jess' wardrobe. "Why do I even know that show? Jess, what have you done to me?"

Flipping through the clothes in Jess' closet, Colin eventually chose – of all things – a flowery sundress that was similar to the one he'd seen Cass wearing a few days ago. He slipped into some comfortable-looking sandals that were anything but comfortable, and brushed Jess' hair. Finally, he surveyed himself in the mirror. Did he look pretty enough to pull off being Jess?

Colin's cheeks immediately went aflame with his thoughts. Jess *was* pretty, and she looked really nice in the dress, but this was hardly the right time to be thinking like that. Then again, she was his sister's best friend, which meant that it should never be appropriate to think like that. He suddenly wished he hadn't noticed.

Jess' mom dropped Colin off at the edge off the park before zooming back down the lane. Colin looked around the park, stepping a little further onto the rich, green grass. There, on a bench beneath a huge weeping willow, sat Ashley, Jen, and Gina. As Colin approached them, they smiled and waved him over.

"Hey, sleepyhead," Gina greeted.

"Hey, girls," Colin said. "I guess I did stay in late."

"Nah, this is early," Ashley said, looking pointedly at her watch.

"Well, anyway, now that you're here," Jen said, "Ashley can tell us her exciting news."

"Ooo, yay!" Colin squealed with all the fake enthusiasm he could muster.

The others girls all grinned at him and Colin groaned inwardly. They leaned into the table, turning their attention to Ashley. Gina clapped her hands and gave Ashley a huge toothy grin, while Jen grabbed Ashley's hand in earnest. Colin didn't know what to do, so he forced a cheery smile and waited.

And waited.

And waited.

"Out with it, girl," Colin finally said, hoping that that was something that Jess would have said.

"Okay," Ashley breathed, clearly not disturbed by Colin's outburst. "I ... like someone."

At first, no one said anything. Then Gina asked, "*Like* like someone?" Ashley nodded.

"Eeeee!!" Gina and Jen screeched together. Colin bit his lip hard and resisted the urge to roll his eyes. *This* was what they were all excited about? Girls...

"Aren't you excited, Jess?" Ashley asked Colin innocently.

Colin smiled. "Of course I am!" he exclaimed in a tone he hoped was taken for sincerity. "But I'd be more excited... if I knew who he was."

"Yeah!" Jen exclaimed. "Tell us."

"I don't know if I should," Ashley said timidly.

"Oh, come on. Why not?" Gina asked. "Ooh, is it someone we know?"

Ashley nodded, chewing her bottom lip thoughtfully. She looked straight at Colin and said, "Okay, promise me you won't tell Cass."

Colin shrugged. "Sure."

"Promise," Ashley insisted.

"I *promise*," he said, giving her a reassuring smile.

"It's Colin," Ashley said. "Cass' brother."

Colin's heart skipped a beat as he stared at Ashley. The other two girls started talking rapidly to Ashley, but Colin didn't hear them. She liked him. She like liked him. She liked him?

"*Why?*" Colin asked, in honest sincerity this time.

"Do you think that's a bad idea?" Ashley asked, her eyes wide.

"It doesn't matter what I think," Colin said, with a confused look on his face.

"Sure it does," Ashley said. "You know him better than I do."

"Not really," Colin lied through his teeth. He smiled coyly and threw in a casual shrug. "I just want to know why you like him. Isn't that what girls are supposed to talk about?"

"Obviously," Gina chirped.

"Alright," Ashley said. "I just... think he's really cute. And he's nice. And," she started twirling her hair around her fingers, "he plays a sport. And I don't know. He's cute."

"He is kind of cute," Colin mused, thinking that Ashley herself was rather attractive.

"You don't have a thing for him, too, do you?" Ashley asked, a look of extreme concern crossing her face.

Colin laughed, a little too loudly. So much for not being conspicuous. "No. Of course not. He's my best friend's brother."

Ashley sighed in relief. "Good. I'd hate to have to fight you for him." She giggled and the other two laughed with her.

Colin faked his laughter, noticing that Ashley now looked slightly less attractive than she did a minute ago.

"Don't worry, Jess," Gina said. "We'll find you a nice boy once school starts."

"Oh, yeah! One with – how did you put it?" Jen added. "Ocean blue eyes and hair the colour of sunshine on a summer day."

Colin's face went flaming red. Had Jess really told them that was the guy she wanted? Why, it almost sounded like Ian, except that it was obvious Cass was in love with Ian. And everyone knows that a girl doesn't go after her best friend's crush.

"Aw, don't be embarrassed, Jess," Jen said. "We all have our secret fantasies."

Now they were talking about fantasies? *Secret* fantasies? Colin couldn't think of one single appropriate response to anything he'd heard in the last five minutes, including Ashley's confession that she liked him. So he clamped his mouth shut and waited for the conversation to move on. Which, of course, took forever, since he was sitting with a bunch of girls.

Their conversation turned to other things, like hair, makeup, and the recital coming up on Friday, but Colin wasn't listening. He was still lost in his own thoughts about how girls were weird because they shared their desires with each other. No guy would ever tell another guy that he wanted a girl with ocean blue eyes and blond sunlight hair. It simply was not done. At least now, Colin knew he wasn't a candidate for Jess' affections.

"You should just tell him," Colin heard Jen telling Ashley.

"I can't," Ashley said. "He'd think I'm weird."

Colin finally decided to put his two cents in and said, "No he wouldn't. Look at you – you're pretty, you're smart, and you dance."

"You think?" Ashley asked timidly.

"Yeah, of course. What could possibly go wrong?" Colin threw in, inwardly grimacing. The only thing wrong with that was that *Colin* was currently *Jess*.

"Like, outright?" Ashley asked, staring inquisitively at Colin. "Maybe I should just kind of hint at it…"

"Yeah, just flirt a lot," Gina suggested.

"No, that won't work," Colin said. "Boys are dumb; they don't get stuff like that. If you get all flirty with him, he'll just think you're being a regular girl."

"I suppose that's possible," Jen said, her voice a bit icy. "But doubtful. You can't just go in there with guns blazing."

"But he won't necessarily know she's trying to flirt with him," Colin argued.

"That's a good point," Gina said. "I mean, Colin is kind of dumb, you know?"

"That wasn't exactly my point," Colin told them, suddenly feeling defensive and trying not to sound like it.

"What would you know about it, anyway?" Jen muttered, but Colin ignored her comment.

"I don't think he's *dumb*," Ashley said. "He's just... not like us."

"What's that supposed to mean?" Colin burst out, his control over his defensiveness weakening.

Ashley gave him a weird look and then said, "Just that he's very athletic. Not necessarily... academic."

"So... you pretty much just like him because he's hot?" Colin asked, his eyes narrowing.

"You think he's hot?" Jen asked as all three girls turned to stare at him.

Colin cleared his throat to stall for time and he could feel red creeping up his neck. He knew he was backing Jess into a corner and he needed to get out.

"Listen, we're way off topic here," Colin finally said. "The point is that you won't get any guy's attention with just a few glances in his directions or even a few flirty comments about his *athleticism*." He directed his last comment to Ashley specifically, and she glanced down uncomfortably.

Jen rolled her eyes. "Seriously, Jess, how would you know anything about it? You've never even had a boyfriend before. What's with all the boy advice?"

"I just –" Colin paused. "I'm just going by common sense, okay?"

"Right." Gina snorted.

"Whatever. I have to go home now." Jen turned to Ashley. "You take whoever's advice you want to."

"I will," Ashley said, surprisingly decisively before casting a brief glance in Colin's direction.

Jen glared at them both and with a flip of her hand walked away from their table. Gina left shortly after, the tension of their final conversation hanging in her goodbye. As soon as Gina was gone, Colin and Ashley got up to walk around the park. It was then that Ashley became a tidal wave of confident chattiness.

"Jess, I've never seen you stand up to Jen like that before," Ashley said. "I mean... like really, never."

"I wasn't really standing up to her," Colin said. "I was standing up *for you*."

"Thanks... I guess," Ashley said.

"Seriously, Ashley. You're a great girl," Colin told her, finding that he meant it. "Why do you let her push you around?"

"I don't," Ashley replied defensively. Colin just looked at her and she half-laughed. "Okay, I kind of do. It's just that Jen and I have been best friends since kindergarten."

"So, it's always been like this?" Colin asked in surprise. These were the kinds of people his sister hung out with? Ashley nodded, almost as if in response to his unspoken question. "Some things don't change, I guess," he said.

"I think she just tries to look out for me, you know?" Ashley said. Colin snorted. "Okay, so maybe she tries a little too hard. But she really is a good friend."

"I believe you," Colin said, even though he didn't. From the corner of his left eye, he saw some younger kids had started up an impromptu soccer game. He stopped walking and stared at them, momentarily tempted to join them.

"What's up, Jess?" Ashley asked when she noticed he had stopped. "Aw, some kids playing soccer. Cute."

"Wow, they need help," Colin mumbled as he watched them run as a group toward the ball, back and forth between the goal posts.

"What's that?"

"Hmm?" Colin snapped out of his reverie. "Oh, nothing. I was just thinking... about playing with them."

"Really?" Ashley scrunched up her nose. "Why would you do that?"

Colin shrugged and forced back the feeling of loss that seeing a soccer game brought him. "I thought it'd be fun."

"Um, okay."

"Plus, I bet if you knew a little about soccer, it would really impress Colin. He's really into it," Colin told her. Finally, something that he didn't have to lie about.

Ashley wavered for half a second and then shook her head. "Nope. Not going to play soccer. Not even for a boy."

She laughed and Colin couldn't help laughing with her. It was worth a shot anyway. He still couldn't believe Ashley *liked* him. He suddenly wondered what Jess would have actually told her if Ashley had had that conversation with her. Maybe he'd ask her when he saw her later.

TEN

After church, Jess discovered that the Jacobses always had lunch with about five or six other families at the local Chinese buffet place. It was like a sacred Sunday tradition. Jess tried not to let it show that she actually had no idea who any of those people were. She avoided names like the plague, and tried not to make lingering eye contact with anyone lest they thought she wanted to converse.

Fortunately for her, everyone who did talk to her mostly kept to safe topics like how Colin was doing with his soccer, and how his grandma was doing. Jess didn't have any problem making up simple answers, even if it meant lying to church people.

Jess secretly texted Colin when she found the chance. Several times, in fact. But Colin never answered, and she was starting to get worried. After what seemed like an eternity, the Jacobs family finally went home.

"Are you going to see Jess today?" Jess asked Cass when they were finally home.

Cass shrugged. "I don't know." She looked at her watch. "She's probably still at the park with the girls."

"Right," Jess said. "The park."

Cass raised an eyebrow. "What, were you waiting for her or something?"

"Me?" Jess tried to put on an air of arrogance. "Pfft, no. I was, uhh... just curious."

"Colin?"

"Yeah?"

"You're getting weirder and weirder," Cass informed Jess. She opened the door to her room, signaling that the conversation was over.

"Yeah, sure," Jess said weakly. "Well, anyway, I gotta –" Cass shut the door on her.

Jess tried not to take Cass' abruptness personally. She knew that was only reserved for Colin, but at the same time, she felt a little bad for Colin. Were things always this tense between Cass and Colin? Just yesterday, they'd gone shopping together, and now Cass was slamming doors in Jess' face.

Jess shook the thoughts from her head. It wasn't her job to fix their relationship, no matter how long she was stuck in Colin's body. She had to get a hold of him. They had to figure this out, and practice more dancing. She decided to go find Colin at the park.

"I guess I should probably go home, Jess," Ashley said to Colin.

Colin nodded, feeling a slight pang of regret now that he was having a nice time with Ashley. But he had to remind himself that Ashley was seeing him as Jess, not Colin.

"Want me to walk you home?" Colin offered, hoping for just a few more minutes with Ashley.

"Nah, that's alright," Ashley said. "But thanks so much for all your advice. It really helped."

As Ashley gave Colin a tight hug, which he happened to enjoy immensely, he asked her, "So are you going to tell him?"

"I think I might," she said, releasing him from the hug. "See ya!"

She skipped off toward the gated exit and Colin smiled after her. Maybe not all of Cass' and Jess' friends were that bad. He could certainly learn to get along with them if it meant spending just a little more time with Ashley.

Of course, that just reminded Colin that he still had to go to Jess' dance rehearsals, at least until they could get back into their own bodies. He wasn't really looking forward to having Jess yell at him for every single movement he made. On the other hand, she still owed him a lot of soccer practice. He decided now was as good a time as any to go find her and mention it to her.

Jess jogged halfway to the park, figuring that it would be good exercise for her since she had to get used to some hard running anyway. When she finally reached the park, she put her hands on her knees and bent over, pulling in large gulps of air. She looked around the park, which was starting to get full with the late afternoon crowd.

She went over to the picnic table her friends usually occupied and checked her watch. The table was empty and she could tell she was too late to catch them. Ashley would have gone home to practice extra dance steps because she was a perfectionist and thought she'd "never get it right." Jen would have left to spend the afternoon with her grandparents because that's what Sunday afternoons were always reserved for. And Gina usually left when Jen left. None of them quite knew why; they only assumed she did it because she considered Jen her best friend.

On the off chance that Colin might still be milling around, Jess decided to scour the park a bit. Unfortunately, Colin wasn't anywhere to be found and disappointment ran through her. She really just wanted to find him, maybe try again to get themselves sorted out. Or at least get him through her dance routine.

"Colin!" a younger boy called from the middle of a field.

Jess jerked her head in his direction and saw that he was surrounded by some of his little friends.

"Colin! Come play with us!" another boy called.

The group was made up of boys between the ages of nine and twelve, and they had momentarily stopped what looked like a mini soccer game to greet Jess as she walked by them. Jess was caught off-guard by their eager faces. They all wanted her, or *Colin* rather, to play with them. It was cute in a way, but she knew that if she tried playing with them they'd know something was wrong right away.

"Thanks, guys," Jess said, holding up a hand. "But I'm kind of looking for someone."

"Who are you looking for?" the first one spoke. He was older and seemed to be the leader of their group.

Jess hesitated, but then decided to come closer to the group. "I'm looking for a girl with blondish hair and green eyes. About this tall," Jess held up a hand to her chin, estimating roughly how tall her body was compared to Colin's. "Skinny and kind of pretty. You seen her?"

The boy looked back at his friends, some of whom started to snicker in the way only young boys do. He looked back at Jess and said, "Yeah, she was with another girl."

"Oh, do you know which way she went?" Jess asked.

"She your girlfriend?" One of the bolder, younger boys asked. Some of the others started laughing and Jess rolled her eyes.

"No," Jess said forcefully. "I just need to talk with her."

"Right," the leader said with a smirk. "She went that way," he pointed toward the exit.

"Thanks," Jess said, starting to jog away. She lifted a hand and threw over her shoulder, "Have fun, boys!"

Jess thought maybe she would just try back at her own house. After all, that was where Colin was supposed to be living while he was in her body. Maybe she'd actually find him there.

After Colin and Ashley split ways, Colin made a mental note to remember Ashley once he was back in his own body. No way did he want to let an opportunity like that go. Ashley was nice, pretty, and from what he'd seen, a good dancer. Then again, he didn't know much about dancing, but it didn't matter.

Colin made his way back to his own home to find Jess. The sooner they got out of this mess, the better. Colin wanted nothing more than to be a boy again, play soccer, and not have girly conversations anymore.

He had to do a bit of sneaking around when he got to his house. He didn't want to let anyone know he was there, especially not Cass. If

Cass saw him, it wouldn't be the weirdest thing, but she'd expect him to come in and listen to her tell him how much she liked Ian and all the blah blah he didn't want right now. He just wanted to find Jess.

Luckily, he still had his late-night sneak-in route in place. All he had to do was climb the tree in the backyard, hop over the little balcony railing and make it to the window before anyone saw. Of course, this was easier done at night when it was dark, but desperate times called for desperate measures.

Jess' body wasn't as strong as his, but at least it was really flexible. Jess was also shorter than Colin, forcing him to re-evaluate his usual method of getting to the balcony. However, Colin managed to climb the tree just fine. He threw Jess' legs over the railing in a most unladylike fashion, but it was the quickest way to go. He came up to his window, peered inside and found... nothing. Or rather, no one. Jess wasn't there.

From outside the window, Colin could hear a tapping on his bedroom door. He quickly shrunk away from view as the door was opened. Colin held his breath as Cass called his name, and then, obviously seeing he wasn't there, shut the door again. Colin let out his breath.

If Jess wasn't there, where was she? Colin took one more glance into the room and, making sure no one saw, he climbed back down the tree. He left the yard exactly as he'd come and started wandering down the street. Should he just go back to her house? Maybe she'd have gone there.

Colin made his way back to Jess' house, trying to stay aware of who was around him. It was always possible that he'd run into her somewhere. As soon as he had reached Jess' front yard, he got a text. It was from Jess and read, "Where in the world are you??"

"I'm at your house," Colin texted back.

"That's impossible," Jess texted. "I'm at my house right now."

"I'm looking are your house, you noob."

Colin entered the backyard silently and found Jess with her thumbs to her cell phone, a look of consternation on her face. She was typing furiously, and Colin couldn't help but smile amusedly at her.

He waited until Jess had sent her text to say, "Jess, I'm right here."

Jess looked up with a startled expression and then she narrowed her eyes. "Where have you been?"

"I had to hang out with your friends at the park," Colin explained.

Jess' eyes widened. "Yeah, but I mean… *Why?*"

"Because I'm supposed to pretend to be you, remember?" Colin answered. "Just like I'm assuming you went to my church this morning. You did go, right?"

"Yes, I went," Jess snapped. At Colin's surprised look, she forced a calm tone in her voice and then said, "Sorry. I'm just frustrated because I didn't know where you were."

"It's alright," Colin said softly.

"My parents aren't home," Jess said, abruptly changing the subject. "We can sit inside for a while if you want."

"Oh, I don't know…" Colin said, giving her a teasing smile. "I'm not sure if I should be alone with a boy in my house."

Jess gave Colin a withering look, but she couldn't help the tiny chuckle that escaped her lips. "You're so silly," she said, making her way to the back door.

Colin giggled and followed Jess into the house. Jess made herself at home in her own kitchen as she searched around the fridge for food. A deep rumble came from the depths of Jess' stomach and she groaned.

"Why are you always so hungry?" Jess whined. "Is there anything to eat in this house?"

"Nothing that will satisfy you in that," Colin said, gesturing to his own body. "You need to keep up your energy. Have you been running? You look like you have."

"Yeah, I have," Jess said, giving him a curious look. "I was running around town looking for you."

"Don't start, Jess," Colin warned. "I climbed up my own tree to my bedroom to find you and you weren't there, so it's not like you're the only one who was frustrated."

"I know," Jess said on a sigh. She pulled some lunch meat and bread out of the fridge. "I just... I don't know how long I can keep this up. Want some?" Out came some lettuce, mayonnaise, and mustard.

"No thanks," Colin said, surprising himself. He didn't feel hungry at all. "You know, it's not exactly easy being you either."

"Well, at least we can agree on that," Jess said distractedly as she spread mustard on a slice of bread.

Colin chose to ignore Jess' comment as she came over to the table with a giant sandwich on her plate. "So, you went to my church, eh?" Colin asked.

Jess bit into her sandwich and nodded. "It was nice," she mumbled.

"Nice? Did anyone notice that I wasn't... quite myself?" Colin asked.

Jess lowered her eyebrows at Colin and swallowed hard. "What do you care about what people think of you?"

"I care very much, thank you," Colin said defensively.

"Okay, sorry," Jess said. "No one seemed to notice. Everyone was super nice to you. Like you were their long lost son or something."

Colin didn't say anything, and Jess gave him a weird look. The truth was that he just didn't want to admit the truth to her and he hoped she wouldn't ask about it. Of course, she did anyway.

"So, what's that all about?"

Colin sighed. "I practically am their prodigal son, okay?" Jess just stared at Colin until he explained, "You know... the son who spent all his inheritance and then... Long story short, his dad was really happy to have him back even though he screwed everything up."

"And this applies to you how?" Jess asked. She took another giant bite of her sandwich.

"Whoa, ease up on the snacking there, Jess," Colin said, stalling for time. He watched Jess chew hardily just for his sake. "I stopped going to church for, like, three years," he finally explained to her. "Then I started going again, and now everyone's happy."

"How come –?"

Colin cut off Jess' question by blurting out, "Your friend Ashley likes me." It wasn't how he'd meant to bring up the topic with Jess, but he also didn't want to answer anymore of her questions.

"No, she doesn't," Jess said calmly.

"Yes, she does," Colin insisted. "She told us."

"What? That's crazy!" Jess exclaimed.

"Thanks," Colin murmured.

"Oh, no, I didn't mean it that way," Jess said. "Of course, we all think you're cute, but–"

"What?"

Jess' face turned bright red, but she ignored his interruption. "But I didn't think any of them liked you. That's all. I didn't mean that you're not likable. Because you are. When you're not being a jerk, you know?"

Colin narrowed his eyes at her. "Jess, just go back to the sandwich."

Jess' face went even redder, if that were possible, and she took yet another bite. "Sorry," she mumbled after she'd finally swallowed.

"Let's just figure this out so I can have a date with a girl that doesn't involve her telling me she likes some guy," Colin said wearily.

"Yeah, okay," Jess said with strained patience. "I know this isn't your favourite thing, but you're not alone in your discomfort, okay?"

"I know."

"So, stop being a martyr."

"Yes, mother."

"Stop."

"Fine."

"Dancing," Jess said, rising from her chair to bring her dish to the sink.

"No, absolutely not," Colin said. "We have so much soccer stuff to work on, and you owe me."

"But I just ate," Jess protested.

"Well, isn't that convenient?" Colin said sarcastically. "That's fine, though. Just bring me some paper and a pen. There's a lot of game play that we need to go over anyway."

Jess sighed and inwardly conceded his point. She did owe him practice time as he'd pointed out. She found Colin some paper and pens and watched as he drew some lines and Xs and Os in what seemed like random spots on the page. Her mind wandered several times as he explained to her what each of the positions where, and she really only caught half of what he'd said. She knew eventually she'd either have to admit that she wasn't listening or fake it.

For now, she'd fake it. She was still holding out hope that they could switch back before Friday. She didn't know how that would happen, but she would try.

ELEVEN

After Colin's long lecture on soccer basics and game play, he and Jess had written each other some rough schedules to get through the next few days in case they couldn't change back. Neither of them really wanted to go through the next week the way they were, but they didn't have a choice. It was either that, or try to explain to everyone what had happened. And obviously, no one would believe *that*.

"Here," Jess said, holding out her cell phone.

It was a pink flip phone with no data plan, and Colin didn't know whether or not he should take it. "Why would I want that?"

Jess rolled her eyes. "Because you'll get lots of calls during the week. And I can't answer them." She shook the phone in front of his face. "Now switch with me."

Colin made a great show of sighing before pulling out his smartphone and handing it over.

"Ooh," Jess cooed, shoving her own phone at him. "What kind of apps do you have on here? Anything fun?"

"Not girl fun," Colin muttered. He picked up the schedule Jess had written and took a closer look. "How do you keep up with this, Jess?"

"What do you mean?" Jess said, distractedly playing with Colin's phone.

"I mean – hey, don't mess with my phone. That's for emergencies only." Colin tried to grab at the phone, but Jess pulled it away from him, never taking her eyes off it. He sighed. "I just meant that your plate is kind of full. Can't I cancel a few of these?"

"No," Jess said, finally looking up at him. "I mean, what would you take out?"

Colin scoffed at her. "You have stupid stuff in here. Lunch with the girls... *every* day. Shopping with Cass? I don't want to go shopping with my sister."

"You did the other day," Jess said with a sardonic chuckle.

"Yeah, about that..." Colin didn't finish his sentence.

"What?"

"What what?"

"What *about* it?" Jess asked, finally setting the phone down and giving Colin her full attention.

"I don't think you should do stuff like that with Cass," Colin said with a shrug. "Not while you're in my body, anyway."

"Why not?" Jess asked. "I *like* shopping with Cass."

"Well, I *don't*," Colin retorted, his voice starting to rise.

"Then learn to love it," Jess said. "Because you know what? She loved it. She loved having her brother do something with her."

That gave Colin pause. He took a deep, calming breath and then asked uncertainly, "She did?"

"You have no idea what it meant to her," Jess said. "I mean, I'll be honest, she probably would have liked going with me better. But she thought it was sweet of you."

"Oh, so, do you feel good about lying to your best friend?" Colin asked bitterly.

Jess narrowed her eyes at him, but she knew she couldn't deny the truth of his words. But that didn't let him off the hook so easily. "Are you okay with lying to *anyone*?"

"This is what it is," Colin said on a sigh.

"Oh, okay," Jess gritted through her teeth. She rose from the table. "Whatever that cryptic reply means. I have to... go."

"Go where?" Colin asked. "Got a hot date?"

"No, I just… have to get away from you right now," Jess answered unapologetically.

Colin watched Jess walk away, his heart sinking with every step she took. When she was almost to the front door, he said, "I don't know what I'm doing."

"Yes, that's quite clear, Colin," Jess said, turning around to face him again.

Colin closed his eyes and then opened them slowly. "I *meant*, I don't know what to do at your rehearsal tomorrow. If we're going to lie to people, then we might as well make it believable."

Jess nodded slowly. "I'll come back tonight, okay?" She reached for the doorknob of the house and then hesitated. She turned back once more to say, "Can you just do me a favour, Col?"

"What's that?" he asked, trying to keep the exasperated tone out of his voice.

"Can you please just spend some time with Cass today?" Jess asked.

Colin wanted to say no badly. It wasn't that he didn't want to be near his sister. It was just that he didn't want to pretend to be her best friend. The lying part bothered him, yes. But he wasn't even sure he'd know how to be her best friend. But then he looked into Jess' eyes – his own eyes – that were silently pleading with him to just get along.

"Fine," Colin finally conceded.

"Thanks," Jess said quietly. "I won't go home for a while so you can hang out with her."

"Where are you going to go?" Colin asked curiously.

"I guess I'm heading to the soccer field," she answered resignedly.

"Jess I –" Colin was cut off by the shutting of the front door. He hadn't meant to offend Jess. He just really *didn't* know what he was doing. All of this was a big mess, and he had no idea how to fix it.

Colin rose resolutely and headed for the front door. Before he left, he looked down at himself and considered the clothes he'd put on that morning. Would Jess have worn these clothes to go see Cass? If he were honest, he'd have to say that he couldn't remember a single thing Jess ever wore when she was over. Deciding that he was being ridiculous and over-thinking things, he left the house and headed to his own.

When Colin got to his house, Cass answered the door with a surprised look on her face. "Jess, hey!"

"Hey, Cass," Colin said, giving her what he hoped was an easy smile.

Cass opened the door wider for him and he followed her into the house. The familiarity of his own home should have put him at ease, but it just made him feel more uncomfortable. How could he ever convince Cass that he was Jess?

"My parents went out, and Colin's off being dumb, I'm sure," Cass informed him. "So we have the place to ourselves. What do you want to do?"

Colin didn't know how to answer. Apparently his sister thought he was dumb, and he had no idea what Jess would have said were she here. So he shrugged and said, "I don't know. What do you want to do?"

"Hmmm," Cass said, tapping a finger on her lips. "I've been wanting to make banana bread."

Colin groaned inwardly. Cass would know in a heartbeat that Jess wasn't quite herself if he was forced to bake something.

He was relieved when she continued with, "But I also rented *Crazy Stupid Love*, and I know you wanted to see that, so we could watch that instead."

"Sure," Colin said. "I'd love to."

"Oh! And I bought a new colour," Cass said enthusiastically. "I'll just go grab it. You can get the movie ready."

"Okay," Colin said. At least he could do that with ease, he thought as he moved into the family room.

Cass joined him just as he was about to get the movie started, holding a small bottle of bright blue nail polish. She sat next to him and smiled. "Are you exited? I think Ryan Gosling has an entire shirtless scene."

"Great," Colin said weakly, barely concealing his grimace.

"I thought you liked him," Cass said, her eyebrows lowering.

"Of course I do!" he answered, trying to fake a girly celebrity crush.

Cass smiled. "Me too. Here, want to do yours first?" she asked, offering him the nail polish.

"Uhh," Colin hesitated. The colour was atrocious in his mind, but what really gave him pause was the fact that he would never be able to put it on himself. Thinking quickly, he said, "Wanna do it for me?"

Cass giggled and said, "Every time," with an amused shake of her head.

Once their nails were done, they both fell silent for a while as they watched the movie. Well, Cass watched the movie. Colin let his mind wander to other things. He wondered if Jess was okay and if she'd really gone to the soccer field. He thought about how if he were himself, he probably would have gone to the field too, but he would have called his friends first. And Jess? Well, she'd be here ogling Ryan Gosling with Cass, and that would have been just fine with him.

Jess hadn't actually been sincere when she'd told Colin she would go to the soccer field, but she found herself magically drawn to it anyway. It must have been Colin's body that brought her there. When she got to the field, she could see a few of his friends playing a five-on-four game. Which meant that if she didn't leave now, she'd get stuck playing with them.

Just as she turned to go, she heard Ian calling, "Col! Come play. We're getting our butts kicked."

Jess pursed her lips and turned slowly back around, knowing there was no way out of this. This was it. It was do or die. She tried to smile at them but knew it probably looked fake. Ian wasn't wearing a shirt, and Jess tried hard not to stare at her best friend's crush's abs.

"Hey, guys," she said.

"Okay, you're skins with me, John, Aaron, and Stan," Ian said by way of greeting.

Skins? Jess didn't want to parade around in Colin's body, let alone half-nakedly playing a sport she barely knew. When she hesitated, Stan ran over and said, "Hey, hurry up. We're losing."

Jess reluctantly pulled her shirt off over her head and tossed in on the pile of other shirts. She made her ways over to the other guys taking their positions, desperately trying not to stare at their sweaty, muscular bodies. *Focus on the game*, she reminded herself.

She ran in to catch up with the others as they proceeded with their game. Jess tried to hold the position that Colin had so painstakingly taught her as she watched them pass the ball back and forth toward the other goal-post.

Ian kicked hard, aiming the ball toward the other goal-post, but the goaltender blocked it with two fists. The shirts came back into play, bringing the ball back toward Jess' side. One of them was coming straight toward her. She held her ground and waited. She was just about to kick the ball away from her opponent, but at the very last moment, she panicked and moved away.

Aaron managed to finagle the ball away from their opponent in time to stop him from trying to score. Jess let out a whoosh of air as Stan narrowed his eyes at her suspiciously. The play started again, and Jess missed another chance to get the ball back into her team's hands.

"Time!" Ian called, making a 'T' with his hands. He jogged over to Jess, who was now breathing heavily from running around and not doing anything right. "Yo, Col, what's going on?"

"Nothing," Jess said. "I'm just… it's been a weird weekend for me, that's all."

"Okay, bro," Ian said, apparently accepting her lame answer. "Just don't sweat it, man. Coach isn't here and there are no girls around to impress.

Jess almost laughed at the irony. Instead she nodded with a small smile. "You're right."

"I'm always right. Now get out there and have fun. This isn't for marks," Ian said encouragingly.

Jess nodded once more and they went back to the others to play again. Jess forced herself to relax and just play. Run, kick a ball, and pretend to be Colin. That shouldn't be that difficult, right?

It turned out that it really wasn't as difficult as Jess first thought. Once she forced herself to remember that it was all just for fun, she was able to loosen up and actually play. It didn't make her miraculously amazing, but at least she was doing better. She stopped freezing up every time an opponent came toward her with a ball, and she even managed to make a few good passes. Maybe she wasn't as terrible at soccer as she had originally thought.

After the game had broken up, Ian followed Jess off the field and they started wandering around town together. Ian didn't speak much, and it reminded Jess about what Colin had told them about their friendship.

"Hey, Colin?" Ian finally spoke up, sounding oddly uncertain.

"Yeah?"

"I want to ask Cass out," Ian said.

"Oh…okay," Jess said, wondering exactly what she was supposed to say in response to that.

"Okay? Okay, like you're okay with that?" Ian asked, his mouth turning up in a smile.

"Uh, well…" Oh, what would Colin say in this situation? "Why?" Jess asked lamely.

Ian shrugged. "She's really pretty."

"That's it?" Jess asked.

"Well, she's nice too, I guess," Ian added.

Jess let out an exasperated breath of air and shook her head. "You want to go out with her because she's pretty and you guess she's nice?"

"Yeah," Ian said, this time more confidently.

"You're kidding right?" Jess said, genuinely concerned.

"No, I'm not kidding," Ian responded, his voice rising just the slightest bit. "And don't act like you're any different. You have the hots for her friend and you know it."

"Whoa, what?" Jess burst out. "I don't –"

"Yeah, you do." Ian smirked. "And you don't have to say it. It's written all over your face whenever she's around."

Jess gasped, but had no words to say. Ian thought Colin liked her? That was just crazy. He couldn't stand her. She rolled her eyes and decided to ignore his comment altogether.

"This isn't about me," Jess said.

"I know. You're right," Ian said. "You're just being protective."

"Yes, I am," Jess said. That, at least, was true. "I don't want Cass to get hurt."

"Who says I'll hurt her?" Ian asked defensively.

"I didn't mean it quite that way," Jess said.

"Look, I know I've had a lot of girlfriends," Ian confessed, "but Cass is different. She's special."

"You're right she is," Jess put in.

"Fine, you don't believe me?" Ian was starting to get angry and Jess didn't even know why.

"No, I wasn't trying to –"

"Whatever, Col," Ian said, holding up a hand. "I don't need your approval. I'm going to ask her out anyway."

"That's fine," Jess replied, feeling her own ire rising at their ridiculous conversation. "Do whatever you want."

"I will." Ian turned to walk in the opposite direction.

"Fine," Jess repeated to his back.

What was with Ian? Jess couldn't figure him out. He seemed easygoing and relaxed, but she'd just managed to provoke him without any warning. All she'd wanted to do was subtly warn Ian that Colin might not be a big fan of him dating Cass. That was all. But clearly, there was no stopping Ian.

Colin got bored about two minutes into the movie. Twenty minutes into the movie, however, he found himself oddly curious as to how

Steve Carell's character was going to navigate the world of dating with Ryan Gosling's help. And just when the movie was getting interesting, Cass decided it was a perfect time to start a conversation.

"Ian called me today," Cass said randomly.

"Oh yeah?" Colin responded, feigning interest.

"Yeah."

Colin waited several moments before asking, "Well, what did he call for?"

"Just to say hi," Cass said. Then she giggled. "He was so cute, too. He told me that he just called to say hi, and then he didn't have anything to say after that, but we were on the phone for like half an hour."

Colin smiled sardonically. That definitely didn't sound like the confident, self-assured Ian he knew. "That's funny," he commented.

"Isn't it, though? He just always seems so... cool." Cass' eyes had gone all googly and Colin had to forcibly refrain from rolling his own eyes.

"Hmm, yeah." What was Colin supposed to say? Ian was his best friend and Cass was his sister. He'd do anything to not have this conversation like this.

"Do you think Colin would be mad?" Cass asked.

"Mad? Over a phone call?" Colin asked, avoiding the actual question. Colin didn't really feel mad, but he still felt like Ian was all wrong for Cass. However, he didn't think he could tell Cass that. Not as Jess.

"I just don't want to drive another wedge between us," Cass said quietly.

Colin clamped his lips shut. Were there other wedges between him and Cass? How had he not known this? He didn't want wedges between them, but apparently she thought there were some.

"What happened between you two?" Colin asked after several minutes.

"We just," Cass paused to force a casual shrug, "drifted, I guess."

"That's it? That's your answer?" Colin asked, trying to keep the indignant tone out of his voice and failing miserably.

Cass drew her eyebrows in thoughtfully and was quiet for another minute. "We just don't see eye-to-eye, Jess. We're into different things." Colin was about to protest her comment when Cass added, "And I mean, he's always making fun of my singing."

"Well, you're not exactly his biggest fan on the field, are you?" Colin asked ungraciously.

Cass narrowed her eyes. "What? Like he's the only one who's allowed to be good at something?"

"That's not what I meant, Cass," he said, wondering how he'd get himself out of this hole.

"Honestly, Jess, if I didn't know any better, I'd say you were taking his side over mine," she complained.

Colin took a deep breath and let it out slowly, mentally calming himself. "I would never," he told her, knowing full well that's exactly what Jess would have said. "Maybe you should make a compromise with him."

"The last compromise I made with him got us both grounded for two weeks," she huffed.

Colin knew exactly to what Cass was referring. One thing they actually did have in common was their favourite book – *The Lion, the Witch, and the Wardrobe* by C.S. Lewis. When they were younger, they had one prized copy of it. One day, while they were fighting over it, Colin suggested that they rip it in half and share it that way. Cass had stupidly agreed and when their parents found out about it, they had both been grounded for not trying to share properly.

"Well, make it a compromise that won't get you in a trouble," Colin suggested.

"Like what?" Cass mumbled.

"Like," he closed his eyes, thinking on his feet, "go to one of his soccer games and he can go to one of your concerts."

"He wouldn't," she argued.

"You never know," he said sincerely.

Just then, they heard the front door open and then slam shut. As heavy footsteps trailed up the stairs, Cass said, "Did I mention his moods?" She let out a disgusted grunt.

"I know," Colin murmured.

He knew perfectly well how moody he could be at times. However, that was not Colin who had come in and slammed the door shut. And now he was wondering what had Jess so upset, but he knew he couldn't go and find out. Not now, anyway. He'd have to wait until later that night.

TWELVE

Colin waited that night for a long time, pacing back and forth in Jess' backyard. She should have known he was waiting since they'd agreed to meet, but she hadn't called or texted him, and he wondered briefly if she was mad at him. However, he couldn't recall a single thing he'd said or done lately that would make her mad enough to not teach him dancing. This was *her* dance recital, after all.

When Colin finally got tired of waiting, he decided to just go to his house and find her. Yes, it would involve more sneaking around, but he had to at least see if she was alright. If something happened to her in his body… what did that mean for him?

His decision made, he headed for his house. It was already after midnight and there were no lights on in the house, for which he was grateful. He slipped into the backyard, climbed up the tree, and hopped over the balcony railing. Careful to not make any noise, he slid the window up and stepped inside his bedroom soundlessly.

Jess was snoring softly in his bed, one leg under the covers and one out. She had on a pair of his shorts and a t-shirt. If it had been him, he would have just been in his boxers, but he figured it wasn't worth mentioning. He watched her breath deeply for a few minutes, thinking that maybe he should just let her sleep.

But then he came to his senses and went over to shake her shoulder. Her eyelids fluttered open as she stretched lazily. And then, as her eyes adjusted to the dark and Colin's face came into focus, she bolted upright in the bed.

"What time is it?" she asked hastily.

"Shh," Colin whispered, putting a finger to his lips. "It's after midnight. What happened to you?"

"I went to lay down around eight," Jess whispered back. "I must have fallen asleep."

"You can't just do that." Colin sank down onto the bed. "I was... I was worried about you when you didn't show up."

"You were worried about me?" Jess asked as she swung her legs over the side of the bed to sit next to him.

"Yeah, about you," Colin admitted. "And me. I mean, what would happen to me if something bad happened to you while you were in my body?"

Jess wanted to be offended that Colin was just thinking of himself, but she couldn't deny the fundamental truth in what he'd said. The same could be said for her in this situation. She took in a deep breath.

"Sorry, Col," she said softly. "I really did mean to meet you tonight. I just felt tired, I guess."

"It's okay," Colin assured her. "I just didn't know what happened, that's all."

"I am sorry," Jess repeated. Colin didn't answer her. "Look, I'm awake now, why don't we work on some stuff?"

"You want to?"

"Sure, why not?" Jess got up to emphasize her point and started for the door to the bedroom.

"No," Colin said quietly, taking her hand to pull her back. "This way." He nodded toward the still-open window.

"You're kidding, right?" Jess peered over Colin's shoulder at the window.

"No, I do this all the time," Colin insisted. "Trust me, my body knows this escape route very well."

"I'm not going to ask why," Jess muttered, following him over to the window.

"Probably a wise decision," Colin answered back as he hooked a leg over the windowsill.

"I can't believe we're doing this," Jess said under her breath as she attempted to follow Colin's exact path off the balcony and down the tree. Though she'd never admit it, climbing down was easier than she'd thought it would be.

"So what'd you do today?" Colin asked conversationally as they made their way through the dark to Jess' house.

"I went to the soccer field like I said I would," Jess answered simply.

"Really? I'm surprised," Colin said.

"I'll be honest and say that I hadn't meant to go there," Jess said. "I guess your body kind of took me there."

Colin laughed. "Some things don't change."

"I guess not." Jess joined in with Colin's laughter. "Anyway, I saw your friends there, so I played with them a bit."

"What?" Colin exclaimed.

Jess tried not to get offended at Colin's outburst and played it cool. "Yeah, it was fun. They made me play skins, though. You should work on your abs."

Colin chose to ignore the abs comment. "Let me guess – it was Ian's choice to play skins, right?"

"Yes," Jess said as she watched Colin roll his eyes. "He thinks he's really hot, doesn't he?"

"Of course he does," Colin answered. He tried to look Jess in the eye, which was hard since it was dark and they were walking side-by-side. "Do you think he's hot?"

"Ugh, Colin," Jess said in an exasperated sigh.

"Well, do you?" he persisted.

"Do we have to talk about this?" she asked, still exasperated.

"I just want to know why Cass likes him so much," Colin said. "That's all."

"So ask her."

"I can't," he argued. "You guys have already had that conversation. She would just tell me that she likes him for all the same reasons."

"Alright, you know what?" Jess stopped walking and turned to face Colin. "He's hot, okay? He's very good-looking." She held out her hand and started ticking off on her fingers. "He plays soccer well. He's confident. And he's nice."

"He's nice?" Colin asked sceptically.

"Yes. He's nice to Cass." Jess watched Colin raise his eyebrows and added, "And he's nice to you, too. Just today, when I was playing horribly, he didn't yell at me or anything. He just told me to chill out and have fun, and it worked. I played a lot better after that."

"What's your point, Jess?" Colin asked.

"I just mean that maybe you should give him a chance," Jess said.

"Jess, he's my best friend," Colin said. "There's nothing wrong between us."

"But you don't want him dating your sister?" Jess asked.

"Absolutely not."

"Well, at least I told him that today," Jess sighed.

"He asked you about it?" Colin asked in surprise.

"Yes."

"What'd you say to him?" he asked.

Jess sighed and shook her head. "I told him... Well, I didn't exactly approve."

"Uh huh," Colin said disbelievingly. "I see."

"Okay, fine." Jess crossed her arms defensively. "He told me that he pretty much likes Cass because she's attractive."

Colin clenched his jaw. "So this whole time you were defending him... what? You didn't mean it or something?"

"I just feel a little conflicted," Jess said. "I'm trying to put together what I knew of him with what you told me and with what I've now come to know about him."

"That... was the most complicated explanation for 'I don't even know this guy' that I've ever heard," Colin said with a little amused grin.

Jess laughed. "Look, it's late. Do you still want me to show you some stuff?"

"Yes please," Colin said. "I don't want to look like an idiot in front of your friends again."

"Especially not Ashley?" Jess teased.

"Not that she'd ever be attracted to me like this," Colin said, "but yeah, especially not Ashley."

"Alright, I'll show you some of the big moves tonight," Jess said. "Just the ones that are used most often. For the other stuff you'll either have to follow along with the girls really well or improvise."

"Whatever you say," Colin said uncertainly.

"Trust me, you'll catch on quick," Jess assured him. "Remember, my body knows these moves."

"Having watched you play soccer, I'm not so convinced that the body knows very much," Colin said.

"Maybe you're not as good a soccer player as you think," Jess murmured.

"Funny girl."

Jess grabbed Colin's arms from behind and started moving them as she counted, "And one, two, three, four..."

Colin tried to follow all of Jess' instructions in the right timing, starting to seriously hope that her body really would remember any of these things. Because he was sure his brain would forget once he awoke in the morning.

Jess woke early the next morning to more of Cass' vocal exercises. They sounded like something of a cross between arpeggios and a dying ostrich, and were followed by a loud knock on Colin's door.

"Colin!" Cass called in a cheery sing-songy voice.

Jess groaned and checked the clock. It was a good thing Cass had knocked on his door because otherwise she probably would have slept right through soccer practice. She just hoped Colin had gotten up for her rehearsal.

As Jess got up and started digging around for some clothes, Cass said through the door, "Colin? Are you up? You should be."

"I'm up," Jess called, pulling on some pants.

"Well, I was just wondering…" the rest of Cass' sentence was too muffled for Jess to hear.

"What?" Jess called, tugging a t-shirt over her head.

"Do you want to come to the mall with me today?" Cass raised her voice. "You can bring your friends."

Jess hesitated. What would Colin have said in this situation? Also, she didn't know if she wanted to spend more time with Colin's friends than necessary. "I don't know if they would really want to come, Cass."

"Sure they would," Cass insisted. "Just come, okay?"

Jess glanced at the clock again. She didn't have time for more debating with Cass. Was this what it was always like between Cass and Colin? Opening up the door, she said, "Fine. I'll see who wants to come. Gotta go, little sister."

"Bye, Colin," Cass said. "Have fun."

Jess hurried out the door with Mrs. Jacobs. She didn't know how well she would play today, and she was extremely nervous. But at least now she knew a little bit more about what she was supposed to be doing in Colin's position. She just hoped that meant the coach wouldn't yell at her again today.

On the field, several of the boys had already shown up and were getting ready. Jess immediately located Ian and went over to him. He was stretching his legs out and Jess joined him, doing some stretches that were more suited to dancing but would still work. Neither of them spoke for several minutes, though Ian knew she was there.

"Hey," Jess finally said.

"Yo," Ian greeted loosely.

Jess stood up and stretched her arms above her head. "I'm sorry about yesterday."

"Don't worry about it, bro," Ian said. "I overreacted."

Ian slapped her on the arm and Jess nodded in what she hoped was a manly manner. And that was that. Coach whistled and with a grin, Ian ran over to the centre of the field with Jess following close behind.

"Okay, listen up, boys," Coach said once everyone was gathered together. "Even though try-outs are *officially* on Friday, you still have four days to impress me. Now get out there and play!"

At his last words, all of the guys standing around started to scatter, some of them instinctively taking the bench, other lining up on the field.

"Jacobs!" Coach called.

It took Jess a moment to realize he was calling her, but she responded as quickly as possible. "Yeah, Coach?"

"I've got my eye on you," Coach said. "You've been playing well all summer long. Don't mess it up now."

No pressure, Jess. Jess swallowed hard and nodded. "Yes, sir."

Coach nodded toward the field and Jess ran to take her position. This time, Jess felt better prepared for what she was supposed to do. It was still a little hard for her to distinguish the invisible lines she wasn't supposed to cross, but at least she knew now when she should and shouldn't try to get the ball. She just hoped Colin's body could handle the rest.

"And-a one, two, three, four," Jess' dance instructor called over the music coming out of the small stereo in a corner of the studio. "Pick-it-up, six, seven, eight. Jess! Two, three, four. What-are-you-doing? Six, seven, eight."

"Improvising?" Colin muttered under his breath.

Colin had tried his hardest to follow along properly. The moves Jess had taught him so far had helped a lot compared to how he'd danced on Saturday. But it was still a challenge. He was tired after last night, and Jess had unfortunately been wrong when she'd said that her body would know what to do. Because it certainly wasn't helping him out now.

Colin's problem wasn't that he couldn't dance, because he'd discovered that he actually kind of could dance. No, the problem was that once he finally got the hang of one routine, they would move on to a different one; one with a completely different tempo and a new set of moves. It was mentally and physically exhausting. If Colin were honest, he might even say it was even more exhausting than playing centre-midfielder.

When rehearsal was over, Colin was just about ready to either lie down and sleep or throw up. He figured whichever one came first was fine with him. But no such luck. The girls were herding him out of the recreation complex before he could even say the words "I'm going to throw up." They were all talking and laughing as they enjoyed the warm sunshine, but Colin lagged behind, not wanting to draw attention to himself.

But Gina saw him and asked, "Are you okay, Jess? You look a little green."

Colin nodded and then ran to a corner of the parking lot where no one was parked. Keenly aware of the others' eyes on him, he threw up what little of the gross shake he'd had that morning. Jess' friends hurried over to him, cooing in concern.

"I'm fine," Colin said, surprising himself with how weak he sounded.

"Are you sure?" Jen asked.

"Are you nervous about the recital?" Ashley asked. "You don't have to be. You're our best dancer."

"Even if you have been doing some weird things lately," Gina said.

"I just haven't been myself, that's all," Colin said, trying to give them a reassuring smile. "Let's go."

"You sure you're okay, Jess?" Ashley asked softly as they all started walking again.

"I'll be fine," Colin said, already starting to feel the queasiness leave him.

Ashley and Colin trailed behind Gina and Jen as they walked the few short blocks to the mall. Ashley spoke quietly to Colin and said, "I know you've been a little off, but you really are our best dancer. Don't be nervous, okay?"

Colin smiled. "Thanks Ashley. I'll try not to be."

"A trip to the mall will cheer you up," Ashley said, returning Colin's smile. "There are always boys there."

Colin suppressed a groan, and with a fake cheeriness said, "Yay."

Cass met them in the mall and immediately clutched Colin's arm as soon as she saw them. Colin was then dragged from one store to the next, from clothing, to accessories, to shoes. If at all possible, this was almost as exhausting as dancing. How did girls keep all of this up and still manage to look pretty at the end of the day? It made him wonder what he looked like, but he dismissed the thought from his mind as being too girly to worry about.

"My brother brought some of his friends by," Cass said conspiratorially to her friends.

The other girls giggled but Colin groaned audibly. Jess had brought *his* friends by? Why would she do that? Of course, Jess' friends thought his reaction was for other reasons.

"Oh, I know he's not your favourite person in the world," Cass said. "But his friends are cute."

"He's kind of cute too," Ashley mumbled.

"I guess he's – they're not bad," Colin said, trying hard not to even think about what he was actually saying.

"That's the spirit!" Jen exclaimed. "Come on, let's go wait by the sports store. I'm sure they must be there."

Colin wasn't sure how to react to any of this. Going all gaga over his friends made him feel extremely uncomfortable, but he knew that staying aloof was not how Jess would have acted. While he pondered his confused thoughts, he didn't even realize they had reached the Sport Chek and he had no more time to decide how to be Jess.

They only had to wait a minute before the boys came out, joking and pushing each other. Colin watched Jess joking and laughing with Ian. Stan and John were next to them, laughing at something that had been previously said. With a pang of jealousy, Colin realized how easily Jess played his part while he was stuck being far removed from his comfort zone.

When Colin's friends saw the girls there, they sobered up a bit and came over. The girls smiled shyly and the boys tried their best to be suave. It was very much like a junior high dance. The only two people not acting ridiculous were Jess and Colin. Of course, they were also the two people who felt the most ridiculous given their particular predicament.

"We were just heading to the food court," Jen was saying. "Do you guys want to come with us?"

"Of course," Ian said, ever the cocky leader.

When they got to the food court, they pushed together some tables and managed to snag enough chairs for each of them. Ashley immediately sat down next to Jess, scooting her chair as close to her as possible.

"Hey, Colin," she breathed close to his ear.

"Hey, Ashley," Jess said. She sent Colin a curious look and he winked at her without letting Ashley see it.

Jess kept as quiet as possible while she watched her friends interact with Colin's and ignored Ashley's attempts at flirting. It wasn't any wonder to her now why Ashley didn't have a boyfriend. Are her lines were ridiculous. Unless, of course, guys actually went for stuff like "I have cherry flavoured lip chap, want some?"

"Hey, I'll be right back," Jess said, mostly to Ashley, who was currently sitting too close to her. "I forgot something I had to do."

"Oh," Ashley said disappointedly. "Want me to come?"

"Nah, it's alright," Jess said with a small, non-encouraging smile. "I'll only be a few minutes."

As soon as Jess started walking away, Colin followed her path with his eyes. A minute later, he got up and followed in her direction. He found her later, hanging out around the corner by a store that neither of them would have gone in.

"Doing a little extra shopping?" Colin asked, gesturing with his head at the Stag Shop next to them.

"What?" Jess looked up at the sign and her face immediately flushed. She laughed nervously. "Obviously not. I was just trying to escape."

"I hear you," Colin said, leaning against the wall next to Jess. "Hey, is everything alright?"

"Other than me not being a very good soccer player and the fact that your friends are pigs, yeah I'm fine," Jess answered. "Oh, and I discovered that one of my best friends has the hots for you, but unfortunately I'm you and she doesn't know. So that's awkward."

Colin had the audacity to laugh. "If it's any consolation, I approve."

"Not funny, Colin."

"Alright, I'm sorry," Colin said. "And I'm sorry about my friends, too. Boys will be boys, right?"

"Whatever," Jess said.

"Plus, your friends are like really weird, too," Colin said.

Jess rolled her eyes. "Come on, let's go back before people see us here."

THIRTEEN

That night, Jess and Colin met and worked separately on their "homework." Jess gave Colin an entirely new list of moves to practice over and over, while Colin set up some markers for Jess to practice her kicking aim.

"I don't know how you do all this," Colin commented as he twisted Jess' body into shapes he'd never known existed before.

"Do what?" Jess asked as she lined up some soccer balls.

"All of it," Colin said. "I mean, I'm exhausted from all of the rehearsals and pretending to be happy and perky with your friends."

"I don't have to pretend to be happy for my friends," Jess said calmly, kicking the first ball and missing the target by a lot.

"You have to keep your leg directed at where you want the ball to go," Colin pointed out.

"Yeah, yeah. Work on your forms," Jess said, her voice edging on frustration.

Colin went back to the list of moves Jess gave him. Some of them were stand-alone while others melded into new ones. It was the transitions that he had the most problems with. Sometimes he just didn't know when to move into a new form or how he should look when he did. Now he understood why there were mirrors all over the dance studio.

Colin was so focused on what he was doing that he was startled when Jess grabbed him around the waist from behind and started guiding his movements. Colin tensed up but Jess didn't seem to notice.

"See, it's like this," Jess said. "Just sway your hips to the right, extend your left arm." When Colin didn't move, she repeated, "Extend your left arm."

Colin cleared his throat nervously and did as Jess instructed. What was wrong with him? Jess was, like, right behind him, practically breathing in his ear and he just couldn't handle it. He turned around and took a couple of steps back.

"Colin, what's wrong?" Jess asked innocently.

"N-nothing," Colin stammered. "Just keep your hands to yourself, okay?"

Jess narrowed her eyes at Colin and then she burst out laughing. "Are you embarrassed or something? I was only trying to help you."

"Yeah, okay, it's fine," Colin said. "Go practice."

Jess gave him one last smirk and then went back to kicking soccer balls. She didn't know what had Colin all riled up, but she had a pretty good feeling he wouldn't tell her anyway. She only half-concentrated on what she was doing because she kept looking back at Colin to see how he was doing. And she had to admit – he didn't look too bad. He just lacked the knowledge. She had no idea how she would ever get him to memorize all of the dances by Friday.

Colin knew Jess was watching him, but he decided not to let on. He wanted to ignore her, but after she'd held onto him and moved his hips that way, he was keenly aware of her presence. He hadn't wanted to admit to her that he'd liked being touched, because it would just make their already awkward predicament even more complicated. Plus it just felt weird.

"Ian told me he was going to ask Cass out," Jess said after they'd been practicing silently for a long time.

"Um, yeah," Colin said. "Actually, he already did."

"Oh."

"Yeah, she told me he did it at the mall today."

"How do you feel about it?" Jess asked.

"I didn't really get a chance to say anything to her," Colin said. "It was kind of a quick mention before she went home with you and I haven't seen her since."

"That's not really an answer to the question," Jess commented.

"I don't really like it," Colin said, trying to keep the emotion out of his voice. "But I didn't know how to tell her without sounding like... me."

"Do you," Jess paused. "Do you want me to talk to her? For you?"

Colin dropped the stance he'd been trying to perfect and turned to look at her. She had also stopped kicking balls to watch him. "You would do that?" Colin asked.

"If you want me to," Jess said. "I mean, she is my best friend, and you know Ian better than me. I could give her a little warning, I guess."

"You really have no qualms about meddling in her business?" Colin asked uncertainly.

"I'm already lying to her, remember?" Jess turned back to the soccer balls.

"Hey, pass me one of those," Colin said, nodding at the other balls on the ground. Jess leaned over to pick one up, but Colin, "No, not like that. Never touch a soccer ball with your hands."

"Sorry," Jess muttered. She haphazardly kicked the soccer ball in Colin's general direction but it went wide by about two feet.

Colin lifted an eyebrow at her. "Did you even think about that before you did it?"

Jess shrugged. "What's there to think about?"

Colin shook his head. "I know you think jocks are stupid and stuff, but there are a lot more cognitive skills involved in sports than you probably think."

"Okay, the fact that you used the word 'cognitive' has my attention," Jess said with a teasing smile. "So educate me."

"You can't just kick something and expect it to read your mind," Colin said. "I mean, it would have even helped you if you were looking at me while you did it, but you weren't."

"Yes I –"

"You weren't," Colin said. "You can't lie to me; I know what I look like when I lie."

"Okay, okay," Jess said. "So I have to look at you. Fair enough."

"And there's a lot of angling involved. Ever play pool?" Jess shook her head and Colin added, "That's okay. My point is that every time you kick the ball, you literally have to make sure you leg follows through in the exact direction that you wanted the ball to go. If not, you're doing it wrong."

"Okay…" Jess said slowly.

She went over to the next ball, lined it up exactly where she wanted it and then kicked it in Colin's direction. She had so much follow through that she actually kicked her leg right out and fell backward on her butt. Colin laughed out loud at her, and she lifted her head to glare at him.

"I'm sorry," Colin said, laughter still in his voice. "But look! You got the ball right to me."

"I did?" Jess asked, sitting up.

"Yup." Colin grinned.

"Woohoo." Jess smiled back at him.

It took all of Jess' energy to concentrate on her soccer playing the next day, but she could see the result of Colin's coaching in her vastly improved performance. It still wasn't quite as good as it should have been and she knew the Coach was keeping his eye on her, as he'd said before, but she tried not to think about that. She just played and tried to have fun like Ian had told her a couple of days ago.

She'd successfully handed off a number of passes to her other team members, particularly Ian, who seemed to know instinctively when to ask her to pass to him. She'd also managed to stop the ball from getting past her defences a few times as well, and she was proud of how much she had improved since Saturday.

But now she realized there was something Colin hadn't taught her: how to actually catch a pass. She missed a number of passes, and the few times she'd caught them, it had been a fluke. One time, she'd even caught a pass but tripped over the ball, and the coach had yelled at her for it.

After the practice finished and the others were slowly packing up and leaving the field, Ian came over to Jess with one eyebrow raised. He looked her up and down, shook his head slightly and then let out a little laugh.

"I don't know what's up with you lately, man," Ian said, "but I decided I'm going to help you."

Jess didn't know whether to feel relieved or offended on Colin's behalf. "You don't have to do that," she said, trying for a polite decline.

"No, I *really* do," Ian said. "I don't want to be on this team without you, so I'm going to make sure you make it on."

Jess hesitated. She had a feeling Colin would hate it if he knew Ian was being all helpful to him, but she also knew that she couldn't keep relying on her late night sessions with Colin to get better at soccer.

Before she got a chance to answer, Ian said, "Come on, dude. Don't let your pride get in the way of taking a little help. You're a good soccer player."

Jess couldn't argue with that logic, so she nodded. "I'd appreciate it. Thanks, Ian."

"Thank me when you get first string." Ian grinned.

Jess smiled back. "I will."

Colin had been sitting with Jen, Gina, and Ashley at Dairy Queen for the last hour. Normally, they would have done milkshakes on Friday, but since that was the day of the recital, they'd moved it up. Colin hadn't said much because he honestly couldn't think of anything to contribute to their conversation. It consisted mostly of boys, clothing, dancing, and famous actors.

"Do you guys ever get tired of dancing?" Colin asked when there was finally a lull in their conversation.

The other three girls turned wide eyes on him and he immediately regretted asking a stupid question. Of course they didn't get tired of it. They lived for dancing.

Jen let out a short little laugh. "You're joking right?"

"Yeah, are you joking?" Ashley asked. "You're not thinking of quitting are you?"

Before Colin could respond, Gina said, "You can't quit. We have a recital on Friday!"

"Have you told Ms. Valmez yet?" Jen asked, referring to their dance instructor. At least Colin now had a name to attach to that particular face and voice.

"What are we supposed to do without you there?" Ashley asked.

"We're not going to quit just because you do," Jen said, a hint of defiance in her voice.

Colin had to get control of this conversation before it got crazy. "Ladies. Calm down. I was just making conversation." As one, the other three let out a relieved sigh. Did they ever do anything apart from each other?

"Yeah, we thought that conversation was leading to you telling us you're quitting," Gina said.

"Why would I quit?" Colin asked. "I love dancing." It was true for Jess at least.

Jen sent a look at the other two girls and then said, "We just thought that…"

"Thought what?" Colin asked, raising one suspicious eyebrow.

"We thought maybe since you haven't been dancing too well the last few days that you were giving up," Jen explained. "Are you?"

"No!" Colin exclaimed. "I told you guys I've just been having a rough time lately. That's all."

"Okay, Jess," Ashley said. "We were just worried. I mean we asked Cass, but she told us nothing was wrong."

"What aren't you telling us?" Gina cut in.

"I can't –" Colin cut himself off and breathed out a frustrated sigh. He *could* tell them, but there was no way he would. "I can't really talk about it right now. I have to go. Sorry."

He stood up abruptly as the other girls gaped at him. They protested and tried to apologize, but he repeated himself and said he had to go. Walking away from their table, he realized he needed the bathroom, so he headed there instead of to the front door of the Dairy Queen.

He'd only been in the bathroom for half a minute when he heard the door open. Two girls were having a conversation and he recognized their voices. It was Ashley and Jen.

"She's just been so weird lately," Jen said. The sound of a stall door opening and closing rang through the bathroom.

"I know," Ashley agreed. "I mean, she gave me love advice. Love advice!" Another stall door opened and closed, and Colin bit his tongue to keep from pointing out how weird it was that they were talking to each other in different stalls.

Jen snorted. "Love advice? Like what?"

Colin stayed in his stall, deciding that maybe he shouldn't come out until they were gone. It was obvious they were talking about Jess – or rather, *him*.

"Well, I was talking to her about Colin," Ashley said.

"Why?" Jen asked derisively.

"'Cause she kind of knows him, right?" Ashley answered. "Anyway, she told me that I should just go right up to him or something and confess my undying love for him."

Colin wanted to say that those were definitely not the words he'd used, but he knew he couldn't.

A toilet flushed and one of the girls walked out of her stall. Jen said, "Love advice from a girl who's never been kissed? That's ridiculous."

"I thought so too," Ashley said, followed by another flush of the toilet. "But it's not like I can just tell her that I think she's wrong. That's rude."

Two taps turned on at the same time and water started flowing. Colin shook his head in anger on Jess' behalf. Why should her friends care if she'd never been kissed? Talk about being rude.

"Yeah well, next time just tell her you don't need her advice," Jen said. "She's always sticking her nose in anyway."

Colin waited until the taps turned off to flush his toilet. The conversation immediately stopped and Colin walked out of the stall with as much confidence as he could gather. He let Ashley and Jen stare at him in an embarrassed silence while he washed his hands.

Just before he left the bathroom, he stared Ashley in the eyes and said, "I was being your friend, Ashley," pointedly.

"I – I know," Ashley stammered.

"Right." Colin spared a glance in Jen's direction and then looked back at Ashley. "So much for not letting Jen push you around."

"What's that supposed to mean?" Jen burst out.

"It means you're manipulative," Colin spit out before rushing out of the bathroom.

Those were Jess' friends? Jen who liked to talk behind her friends' backs and Ashley who could be one way to your face and completely different with someone else? What had Jess ever seen in them? What had he ever seen in Ashley?

"Where are you?" Colin texted to Jess.

A few minutes later, she texted back, "Just leaving the soccer field. Ian practiced with me for a few."

Now, on top of all of that, Colin got to feel jealous that Jess was spending extra time with *his* best friend. That was just great. Jen's friends were jerks. He might not approve of his sister going out with Ian, but at least with Ian, what you saw was what you got.

Disgusted with Ashley and Jen, Colin stalked out of the Dairy Queen and practically speed-walked all the way back to Jess' house. When he got there, he shut himself in her room. Jess' phone went off a few times, but he ignored it. He wasn't ready to tell Jess what had just happened. And if it was one of Jess' friends, he definitely didn't want to talk to them.

Colin flopped down onto Jess' bed and put his arm over his eyes. He knew he shouldn't have walked out of the bathroom stall like that or said the things he had, but he couldn't help it. He had to defend his – or rather, Jess' – honour. Regardless of the fact that those girls were supposed to be Jess' friends and he still had to dance with them.

A knock sounded at the door and Colin said, "I'm not hungry."

"Good, 'cause it's not room service," came a voice from the other side. It was his voice. It was Jess.

Colin got up from the bed, opened the door, and let her in. "What are you doing here, Jess?" He whispered.

"I've been texting you for the last hour and you didn't respond," Jess whispered back. Then in a full voice, she asked, "Why are we whispering?"

"Do you want your parents to think you're alone with a boy in your room?" Colin asked in a low voice.

Jess shrugged. "They went out. I watched them leave a few minutes ago."

"Well, that's not stalkerish at all," Colin said sarcastically, flopping back down on the bed.

"What's wrong?" Jess asked.

"I don't want to tell you," Colin mumbled.

"Is this about the dancing?" Jess asked gently.

"No," Colin answered. "Although, that could be going better, I admit."

"Is it... about the period thing?"

"No!"

"Then what?" Jess persisted.

"It's your friends," Colin said.

"What about them?" Jess sat next to Colin's outstretched body on the bed.

"Look, the other day," Colin started his explanation, "I gave Ashley a little advice about talking to a certain guy."

"Okay…"

"And then she turns around and tells Jen about what I said, but she blew it all out of proportion," Colin explained.

"So far, I'm following you," Jess said.

"Right," Colin said. "So I overheard them talking about it in the bathroom today. And you know what Jen said?" He put on a weird voice and said, "Oh Ashley, I can't believe you took love advice from a girl who's never even been kissed."

Jess' face went bright red. "She said that?" she asked weakly.

"Yes!" Colin exclaimed. "Which, if you ask me, isn't even any of her business. I mean, why would you even tell someone that?"

"It's kind of hard to hide when you've never had a boyfriend," Jess said shyly.

"Sorry," Colin said softly. "It's not that, though. What bothers me is that Jen's manipulative and Ashley's a sheep. Doesn't that bother you, too?"

"A little bit, I guess," Jess said. "But I've known them for so long. It's hard to stop being friends with people sometimes, you know?"

Colin snorted.

"Why do you think Cass is my best friend?" Jess asked. "Because she's not like them."

"Well, that's good to know." Colin knew he should tell Jess about what he'd said to Jen, but he didn't know how to break it to her. "Jess, there's something else…"

"What?" Jess asked, dreading the answer.

"I kind of… told them off," Colin said slowly.

Jess sighed. She didn't know how to respond to that. Slowly she stretched out on the bed next to Colin and laid her head on the pillow beside his. He scooted over for her and they were silent for a few minutes.

"Are you mad at me?" Colin asked quietly.

"No," Jess said. "I guess that was a long time coming."

There was another beat of silence.

"Thanks," Jess said.

"For what?" Colin asked.

"For defending me, I guess," Jess said.

"You deserve it," Colin answered, finding that he actually meant it.

FOURTEEN

Jess left her house in time to make it to the Jacobses' house for dinner. As she walked there, she thought about what Colin had said. She'd known what Jen was like for a long time, but Ashley too? Although she hadn't said it, Ashley's betrayal stung, particularly since they'd spent long hours complaining about Jen's gossiping streak.

Colin had defended her. She wondered if he'd done it for her or for himself. It was hard to say, but a part of her wanted to believe that he'd done it for her. It warmed her heart to think of it that way.

When she got into the house, she heard singing along with piano accompaniment behind it. It was Cass' voice. Jess followed the music into the den where Cass was sitting at the piano. This was a first for Jess. She'd never known that Cass could play piano. Granted, the piano-playing wasn't quite as good as her singing, but it didn't need to be. Cass' singing out-shone everything else.

Jess stood just inside the doorway of the den and listened to Cass finish the song. When she was done, Jess clapped for her. Cass whirled around on the piano stool and looked at Jess with surprised eyes.

"How much of that did you hear?" Cass asked breathlessly.

"Enough," Jess answered with a smile. "You're so good."

"I thought you were out," Cass said.

"I just got in," Jess answered. Her eyebrows drew in. "Are you hiding your music from me or something?"

Cass started to walk past Jess as she said, "You make fun of it, Colin. Don't expect anything better."

Colin made fun of Cass' music? That wasn't nice. As long as Jess was in his body, she might as well make things better for him.

"Wait, Cass." Jess waited for Cass to stop walking and then said, "I'm sorry that I do that. I don't mean it."

"Then why do you do it?" Cass asked.

"Because… I'm a boy and boys are idiots?" Jess supplied. At least that much she thought was true.

Her excuse made Cass smile a little. "They're not all idiots."

Jess chose not to ask to what or whom Cass was referring. Instead, she asked, "How long have you been practising piano?" at the risk of giving herself away.

Apparently Jess had guessed correctly that Colin didn't know about Cass' piano playing, because Cass didn't seem surprised that Jess didn't know.

"Just over the summer," Cass replied. "Mom and Dad got me signed up for lessons and I practice at home when…"

"When?"

"When you're gone," Cass finished with an uncomfortable shrug.

"Cass, you don't have to do that," Jess said. "You sound really good. I promise I'll stop bugging you about it."

Jess knew she shouldn't make such wild promises on Colin's behalf, but it was worth the lie to see Cass' face brighten the way it did. Cass was about to go again, but Jess stopped her once more.

"Play something for me," Jess said, trying to keep her voice even so she didn't sound too eager but didn't sound bored either.

Cass hesitated, then with a grin made her way back to the piano. "What do you want to hear?" she asked.

"Your best song, of course," Jess said, sitting down cross-legged on the floor next to Cass.

"I don't really know what my best one is," Cass said shyly.

"Yes, you do," Jess said. She nudged Cass' leg.

"You're right. I totally have a best one." She shuffled around some of the papers on the piano stand and finally pulled one out in front. "It's from *The Phantom of the Opera*," Cass explained. "It's the part where she goes to her father's grave, and it's all sad and stuff."

"Right," Jess said, even though she'd never seen *The Phantom of the Opera*. "And you like it because…?" She left the question open-ended.

"Because even though it's sad, it's still really pretty," Cass said.

Jess made a motion with her hand that clearly said "Get on with it." Cass took a deep calming breath, positioned her fingers over the keys and then started to play. She stumbled over a couple notes in the intro, and the rhythm was halting, but when she started to sing, the song took off.

Cass was right: the song was both sad and beautiful. It also suited her voice wonderfully, which was probably another reason why Cass liked it so much. Jess had never heard any of the songs until now, but the way Cass did it made Jess want to hear all of the music. When Cass played the final chord, Jess clapped.

"I know it's not great," Cass said.

"No, it was amazing." Jess was hardly able to keep the excitement and awe out of her voice.

"You really think so?" Cass asked.

Jess nodded enthusiastically but was caught off-guard when a voice from the doorway said, "Well, this is new."

Both Jess and Cass turned to see Mrs. Jacobs gazing fondly at her two children. Jess stood up as Mrs. Jacobs stepped inside the room and said, "This looks an awful lot like you two getting along."

Jess gave Cass an amused look and said, "It would seem that way."

"It would seem that way?" Mrs. Jacobs laughed. "Who are you and what have you done with my son?"

Jess laughed nervously even though she knew that Mrs. Jacobs was definitely joking. Hopefully.

"I was just doing one of my songs for Colin," Cass said.

"You sounded beautiful, my dear," Mrs. Jacobs said kindly.

"Thanks, Mom." Cass beamed.

"Is it dinnertime yet?" Jess asked, trying to get back into Colin's role.

"There he is," Cass said wryly.

Mrs. Jacobs nodded and laughed. "Well at least I got to see you two being nice to each other once more before I died."

At that both Jess and Cass laughed.

Colin sat quietly at the dinner table with Mr. and Mrs. Lewis. Normally, he felt awkward having such a subdued dinner, since it was never like that for him at home. But tonight, he didn't mind. Even though his little talk with Jess had helped a lot, he was still brooding over Jess' friends. Jen he could see as the back-stabber type. Ashley, on the other hand? To think she'd been so sweet with him and then said those mean things about Jess behind her back.

Colin's emotions must have shown on his face because Mrs. Lewis asked, "Is something wrong, Jessica?"

"No," Colin muttered.

"Are you sure?" Jess' mom persisted.

"If you must know," Colin said with a hint of indignation, "my friends are manipulative back-stabbers who don't know when or how to keep their opinions to themselves."

Mrs. Lewis exchanged a glance with Mr. Lewis. It was obvious Colin had shocked them with his announcement. Unfortunately, he had no idea what Jess was like with her folks, so he had no model to follow in this circumstance. He just figured honesty, to a certain point, was the best policy.

"What exactly happened?" Mr. Lewis asked, finally showing some sign that he was actually listening to Jess.

"Nothing." Colin shook his head. "I just overheard a couple of them talking about me today."

"What did they say?" Mrs. Lewis asked, all her motherly protective instincts ready to pounce at a moment's notice.

"It doesn't really matter," Colin said, touched that she was so ready to defend him, even if she wasn't his real mother. "It was just really mean. That's all."

"Well, what are you going to do?" Mr. Lewis asked. He was clearly a go-getter.

"It's not what I'm *going to do*," Colin said with a sigh. "I already told them what they said was really mean. And that I thought they weren't being good friends."

Mr. Lewis nodded with a small smile on his lips. "Good for you, Jessica. I'm really proud of you."

Colin smiled back. "Thanks. I'm proud of me, too."

That night, when Jess came over to practice with Colin, she insisted on making him mirror her dance moves, saying that that would be the quickest way to learn them. For once, Colin didn't complain. He still felt bad that Jess had been so poorly treated by her friends. Or at least, she would have been, if she'd been in her own body. Either way, he still thought they were rotten girls.

"Quick question," Jess said, as she watched Colin extend his arms out as she did. "Did you by any chance know that Cass plays piano?"

Colin waited a beat, followed Jess' movement, and then answered, "Yes, actually."

"How'd you find out?" Jess asked.

"I've known for a while. I walked into the house once and heard her playing," Colin explained. "Actually, I did that a couple of times before I figured out that she only practiced when I wasn't home."

"And you never told her." It was statement, not a question, since Jess knew for a fact that Colin hadn't told her.

"No, she doesn't know that I know," Colin said.

"Umm…" Jess hesitated. "She kind of… does now."

"Oh."

"Is that okay? I didn't know that she didn't know that you knew," Jess said all in one breath.

"It's alright, I guess," Colin said, not sounding in the least bit worried or mad. "It was bound to come out eventually."

"I heard her playing and it was so good, so I went in and asked her about it," Jess explained. "And then she sang me a song from *The Phantom of the Opera*."

Colin nodded. "It's her best one."

"That's what she said, yeah," Jess said happily. "How come you make fun of her music?"

Colin dropped the stance he'd been doing and said defensively, "I don't."

"She seems to think you do," Jess answered, also dropping the movement she was showing Colin.

"Well, I might have once or twice…"

"You *might have* enough for Cass to think that you do all the time," Jess argued. "And I think maybe… you're the reason she's so afraid to share it with people."

"No," Colin said, more confused than upset. "She's afraid because she's shy."

"She's not shy," Jess said with a shake of her head. "She's never been shy."

Colin had no answer to that. He bit his lip as he thought about Jess' words. She was right, Cass wasn't a shy girl. And maybe he had teased her a few too many times. But was that really the reason she didn't want to tell people that she played piano?

"Colin," Jess cut into his thoughts, "I don't mean to overstep my boundaries here, but… a lot of what you do affects Cass. Do you even realize that?"

"No, I guess I didn't," Colin said quietly. "I always kind of thought you were more influential in her life than anyone else."

Jess shook her head. "No. It's definitely you."

"Why me?" Colin asked.

"Because you're her big brother. You're her role model," Jess said. "And if she can't look up to you, who's she supposed to look up to? Her dumb friends? Her out-dated parents?"

Colin cleared his throat, signaling that Jess was getting out of the comfort zone area of their conversation. Jess, however, wasn't willing to let him off the hook just yet.

"Look, it's obvious you care about her. Otherwise, you wouldn't be so touchy about the whole Ian thing," Jess said.

"I'm not touchy," Colin said in a defensive tone, disproving himself.

"Yes, you are," Jess answered. "But that's not my point. My point is that if you really do care about her, maybe you should take the time to actually listen to her. Bond with her."

"Bond with her?" Colin asked. "How am I supposed to do that?"

"That, you'll have to figure out on your own." Jess sent him an apologetic smile. She knew she'd gone too far tonight, but at least Colin hadn't gotten angry. With an abrupt subject change, she got back into a dancer's stance and started counting.

"By the way," Jess said after a few more minutes of silent, mirrored dancing, "Ashley really is a sheep. I could have told you that a long time ago."

"But you didn't," Colin said dryly.

"No. Some lessons are better learned the hard way." Jess smirked. "There's always the granddaughter of that old lady at church."

"Mrs. Abernathy?" Colin asked. "How do you know about her?"

"I helped her get a box down from a shelf on Sunday and she told me her granddaughter was coming down this weekend," Jess told him. "I think she's trying to set you two up."

Colin started laughing uncontrollably. At first, Jess joined in with some confused laughter, and then when she'd had enough, she asked, "What's so funny, Colin?"

"Oh, nothing," he answered, wiping laughter tears from his eyes. "Some lessons are just better learned the hard way."

"I'm not sure I should even pretend to know what you're talking about," Jess said.

"Probably for the best," Colin replied, still chuckling.

FIFTEEN

After Wednesday's dance rehearsal, Colin had chosen not to go out with the girls after. Jen hadn't said a word to him, but Ashley had tried to talk to him a couple of times. Each time, though, he'd told her that he just needed some space. Gina was the only one who he didn't have a grudge against, so he walked away from the recreation complex with her.

Gina wasn't her usual bubbly self and Colin wondered if maybe Jen or Ashley had said something to her. His suspicions were confirmed when she finally said, "Ashley told me what happened yesterday in the bathroom."

"Yeah?" Colin responded. "Did she tell it from her point of view or Jen's?"

Gina sighed. "You're being a little hard on Ashley, aren't you?"

"You know what I mean though, right?" Colin asked.

"Yeah, I do," Gina said. "But she did try to apologize to you like a hundred times today."

"A hundred might not be enough," Colin said.

"It's not like you to hold a grudge," Gina said gently.

Gina was right; Jess would never hold a grudge. Colin himself didn't usually hold grudges either, but it was still bothering him. But he knew eventually that he'd have to at least forgive Ashley for Jess' sake.

"You're right," Colin finally conceded. "I'll talk to her. But not yet."

"Good," Gina said. "Hey, where are we walking to?"

Colin looked around him and smiled at the familiarity. He'd been heading in the direction of the soccer field out of force of habit without even realizing it.

"We're going to the soccer field," Colin said.

"What? Why?" Gina asked.

Colin didn't really have an answer. A part of him just wanted to see Jess; the rest of him was just heading there for the sake of being somewhere he felt comfortable. So he lied and said, "To check out the soccer players, of course."

Gina giggled. "Why didn't I think of that?"

Colin giggled too, and the two of them walked the rest of the way to the field. When they got there, the practice was still happening. Colin guided Gina to a bench on the bleachers and together they watched the practice finish up. While Gina pointed out random guys saying, "He's cute," Colin's eyes were keenly fixed on Jess.

Jess wasn't a perfect player, but he could tell she'd learned a lot and she was putting a lot of effort into what she was doing. He admired her tenacity on the field. When Coach yelled at her, she didn't even bat an eye; she simply adjusted her play and moved forward. Maybe there was hope for her after all.

Coach blew the final whistle and the guys, sweating and breathing hard, jogged back to the bench to gather all their stuff. Some of them took their time with long mouthfuls of water, while others horsed around with each other.

"I'm going to go flirt," Gina announced. Then she stood up and, with all the confidence in the world, walked down to where a group of guys were standing and joking with each other.

Colin shook his head with an amused chuckle. He looked back to where Jess was and she was staring at him. When he saw her, she waved, and he made a hand motion for her to come talk to him. Jess climbed halfway up the bleachers and sat down hard next to him. Colin could tell she was tired.

"You've gotten so good," Colin complimented.

"Thanks," Jess said with a smile. "I'll never be as good as you probably are, though." There was a sadness in her tone of voice.

Colin nodded. "If it's any consolation, I could never be as good a dancer as you are."

"Hmm, that's not really a consolation," Jess said. "Especially since you're supposed to dance for me in two days."

"Good point."

They fell into a silence as they watched the other guys winding down and getting ready to go. Gina was still down there, chatting a million miles a minute. She'd managed to captivate their attention well enough that no one really noticed Jess and Colin on the bleachers.

"How is…" Jess wasn't quite sure how to finish her question. "How is everything with everyone else?"

Colin sighed and shook his head. "Jen wouldn't even look at me today. Ashley tried talking to me a billion times, but I was still too mad at her. Sorry, Jess. I guess I kind of ruined things for you."

"It's okay, Colin," Jess said softly.

Colin shook his head. "Your friends are so wrong about you."

"Yeah?"

"Yes," Colin insisted. "You're like this amazing girl who would always stick up for her friends, always stand up for what she believes in, and always do what's right. I don't see anything wrong with that."

"Colin," Jess breathed, feeling heat rising to her face. Where had all that come from?

"Don't argue with me, Jess," Colin said, mistaking Jess' tone. "It's all true. Your friends are just dumb. Although, seeing my friends from a girl's perspective right now, I'd have to say they're kind of dumb, too," he quipped.

Jess laughed. "Nah, they're alright Colin. But I have to say, Ian is getting a little too flirty with Gina."

"I told you," Colin said. Then, out of nowhere, he asked, "Why do your friends care when or by whom you've been kissed?"

Jess shrugged uncomfortably. "Like you said, they're just being dumb. Don't worry about it."

"I'm not worried about it," Colin said. Then he turned to her with this look on his face that Jess knew meant that *she* should be worried. "You know what you should do? You should pick a guy and kiss him."

"What?" Jess exclaimed.

"Yeah, just pick a guy your friends think is cute and kiss him," Colin said. He smiled encouragingly like his plan was fool-proof.

"And when am I doing this exactly?" Jess asked sceptically.

Colin looked down at where several of the soccer players were still lingering. Gesturing with his thumb, he said, "Plenty of witnesses here now."

Jess glanced at them briefly and said with an amused smile, "You realize that means *you'd* have to kiss one of them, right?"

"Oh," Colin said, finally realizing the error in his "brilliant" plan. "Well, that would be extremely awkward. Forget I said anything."

"I appreciate you trying to help me," Jess said. "But yeah, that wouldn't have worked. Unless..."

"No, really," Colin said. "I'm not going to kiss one of my friends, so forget it."

"Not *them*, Colin," Jess said. "*Me*."

"What?"

"My friends think you're cute," Jess explained. "I'll kiss you. Or... you kiss me. Whatever way you want to look at it."

Colin took a good long look at Jess and finally decided that she was, in fact, serious. "You want to kiss me?"

"I want..." Jess paused to consider her words. "I want it to look like you're kissing me."

"Umm..." Colin hesitated. He scratched his head to stall for time and then looked down at the dwindling soccer players. "Okay," he finally said.

Jess moved closer to Colin on the bench and slowly leaned her head down. Colin swallowed nervously as Jess closed her eyes. Then, just at the last moment, he put his hand on her chest and gently pushed her back a bit.

"Wait," he said.

"Too weird?" she asked.

"It's not that," Colin said. "Well, it's not *just* that."

"Then what?"

"This isn't as good an idea as I thought," Colin said in a lame attempt to explain himself. "I just think your first kiss should be with someone you care about."

"I do care about you," Jess said softly.

"I mean someone you really like," Colin added.

Jess knew Colin was right. At the same time, however, it struck Jess that she actually really did like Colin. After all these days they'd spent as each other, it turned out he wasn't as bad as she'd originally thought. But it was obvious that Colin didn't feel the same way, or else he wouldn't have said anything. She tried not to let the hurt show as she moved away from him.

"I'm sorry," Colin was saying while all these thoughts were swirling around Jess' head. "I don't deserve to have your first kiss."

"I understand," she said under her breath.

"Are you mad?" he asked in a concerned tone.

"No," Jess said, giving him a reassuring smile. Mad wasn't quite the word for it. Disappointed was more accurate.

Colin wanted to say more but he didn't know what he should say. Looking down at the last few people on the field, he saw that Gina was watching them. He stood up.

"I think Gina's waiting to go," Colin said. Jess wouldn't meet his eyes. "I'm sorry. This whole thing is just so out of hand, you know?"

Jess nodded. She looked up at him with a complacent smile that shot straight through his heart. "See you tonight?"

"Of course," he said.

He looked back at her a couple of times and almost tripped down the bleachers. She looked sad. That wasn't good. Making girls sad was never good, but there wasn't much Colin could do about it now. He waved to her after hopping off the last step and she sent him a little wave in return.

"Ready to go?" Colin asked Gina, who was just saying goodbye to the few remaining soccer players.

"Are *you* ready to go?" Gina asked, giving Colin a knowing look.

"Yes," Colin answered, ignoring the implication.

When they had left the soccer field, Gina asked, "So what was all that about back there? Are you trying to get back at Ashley?"

"What are you talking about?" Colin asked, genuinely confused.

"I'm talking about your one-on-one with Colin Jacobs on the bleachers," Gina said.

"That was nothing," Colin told her, even though they'd almost kissed. But there was no point in telling Gina that now.

"You looked pretty cozy to me." Gina smirked.

"We're just friends," Colin insisted. "Nothing more. I mean, he's Cass' older brother. It would never happen."

"Right," Gina said disbelievingly. "You obviously didn't see the way he looked at you, then."

"The way he looked at me? How did he look at me?" Colin asked uncertainly.

"Oh you know," Gina said. "He was all googly-eyed, like he's never seen a pretty girl before you. He didn't even notice when we all called his name. Then again, neither did you."

Colin couldn't believe what Gina was telling him. Jess looking at him with "googly eyes"? No. That wasn't possible. He was sure that everything he'd said about Jess not liking Colin was true. Gina had obviously mistaken their warped conversation for something else.

"I don't think it is what you think it is," Colin said.

"Say what you like, but I know what I saw," Gina responded.

"So you're getting on me because of my *one* conversation with *one* guy?" Colin asked. "When you yourself were flirting with, like, ten million guys?"

"The difference is that I never denied it," Gina said, tossing Colin a coy smile.

"Fair enough," Colin said with laughter in his voice.

When Jess finally climbed off the bleachers, there still one person left on the field. It was Ian. Jess groaned inwardly, hoping that he wouldn't make her play more soccer with him. It was nice that he wanted to help, but she was all soccered out.

"Dude, that Gina chick is really cool," Ian said.

"Yeah, she is," Jess said, wondering where Ian was going with that line of thinking.

"She dances with Jess, too, doesn't she?" Ian asked.

"Yup," Jess answered.

"She's really pretty, too," Ian said.

"Yeah, she's pretty," Jess said, starting to get a little exasperated. "Gina's pretty, and Jess is pretty, and Cass is pretty."

"So many pretty girls," Ian said with a dreamy smile.

"Aren't you going on a date with Cass tomorrow night?" Jess asked, her face scrunched up in obvious disapproval.

"Yeah. What's your point?" Ian asked with a raised eyebrow.

"My point is try to keep one pretty girl in your head at a time, okay?" Jess said, shaking her head slightly.

"Okay, Colin," Ian said. "Don't get so offended. I was just saying."

"Okay, I'm sorry," Jess said. She smiled in a gesture of goodwill. "So… soccer try-outs soon, eh?"

"Yeah, man," Ian said easily, apparently accepting Jess' proffered olive branch. "You should make sure you eat enough."

Eat enough? What was that supposed to mean? Jess decided to ask Colin later. "Yeah, you too. I'll catch you later."

"See you, Colin," Ian said as he started jogging away from Jess.

Jess sighed in relief. She probably shouldn't have been so hard on Ian, but she was beginning to see why Colin was been worried. In fact, she was beginning to see a lot of things the way Colin did. And it scared her. She wondered if maybe she was really going to be stuck in his body and always have to see things as he did.

Thinking about Colin reminded her of their near-kiss earlier. How foolish could she have been to think that Colin would actually want to kiss her? And while she was in his body, no less! She still couldn't believe she'd made such a stupid suggestion to him. Now he would feel all awkward around her and not know what to say, and so she would feel awkward and not know what to say either. When did she become so good at messing things up? Maybe it was when she turned into Colin, she thought with a wry smile. That would explain a lot.

Contrary to what Jess had expected, that night Colin didn't act the slightest bit awkward with her. So if Colin felt weird at all, he wasn't letting it show. In fact, Colin was being nicer to her than she'd ever known him to be. Which was just fine with Jess.

What Jess didn't know was that Colin didn't even realize he was being so nice to her. Somewhere over the last couple of days his feelings and his attitude toward her had changed. She was no longer "Jess, Cass' annoying best friend." She was now "Jess, the only girl who could be in this situation with him and still hold her head high." And there was something attractively admirable about that.

"I guess I see now why you didn't really want Cass to go out with Ian," Jess cut into his thoughts.

"Oh yeah? Why's that?" Colin asked distractedly.

Jess put a hand on her hip and pursed her lips. "Wow. You really haven't been listening to me for the past five minutes, have you?"

"Uhh, I guess not," Colin said with a chuckle.

"Were you just really concentrated on dancing, or do you have something else on your mind?" Jess asked.

"Both," Colin replied cryptically, not wanting to admit what he'd really been thinking about. "I'm sorry. Please tell me what you said."

Jess shook her head with a little amused smile, and repeated her whole story about her conversation with Ian that afternoon. She finished her story with, "What are we going to do?"

"What are we going to do?" Colin repeated, like the words Jess had said were foreign to him.

"Yeah," Jess said. "Don't you think we should do something?"

Colin shook his head. "What's there to do? They're going out tomorrow. They'll talk, and laugh, and have fun. We can't really stop that."

"But —"

"You said it yourself, Jess," Colin said. "Some lessons are better learned the hard way. You and I have already done our parts."

"Fine," Jess said in a resigned tone of voice. But she wouldn't give up just yet. There was still some hope.

SIXTEEN

Jess awoke the next morning to Colin's phone going off next to her. It was a text from him that read "Last day good luck!" and despite its lack of punctuation and the early hour at which Colin had sent it, it warmed her heart.

She texted back, "Break a leg!"

Colin sent back, "Don't break any of mine."

Jess chuckled to herself and lay her head back against the pillow and fell back asleep. Soccer practice was still a couple hours away, so she figured she would get the extra rest.

Colin, on the other hand, was up and ready to go before he had even sent his text message to Jess. Even though he and Jess had stayed up late to practice, he felt well-rested and ready to take on the day. Today was an important day, maybe even as important as tomorrow would be.

Colin felt good. He stretched, warmed up, and dressed in dance clothes while he waited for Jess' mom to get ready. He even took the time to put Jess' hair up in a perfect bun, as he'd noticed that was what most girls did while they were dancing. He understood why now: it was so much easier to dance when he didn't have hair whipping all over his face.

He got to the recreation complex early, which was unusual for him. Or maybe it was usual for Jess, but he wouldn't have known that. Jen was leaning against the wall outside the door of the studio looking bored and aloof. When she saw Colin coming, she straightened up and met Colin's icy gaze.

"Hey, Jess," Jen greeted, trying for a friendly smile. But Colin wasn't buying it. He put his hand on the door to go in, but Jen stopped him. "Wait, don't. I have something to say first."

"So, say it," Colin snapped.

Jen was momentarily taken aback by Colin's tone, but she recovered quickly. "I'm sorry."

"Okay," Colin said. Again he reached for the door, and again Jen stopped him.

"I shouldn't have said those things about you," Jen said. "I was out of line."

"You're right," Colin said. "You shouldn't have said those things about me."

"And I'm sorry," Jen said.

"But you also shouldn't be thinking those things about me," Colin added, ignoring Jen's repeated apology.

"What?" Jen asked.

"I said, you shouldn't –"

Jen cut him off. "I heard what you said. I just don't know what you mean by it."

"Anything you think will come out in what you say," Colin explained. "So I'm just wondering why I should still be friends with someone who thinks those things about me."

"I – I," Jen stammered. Her line of vision dropped and she shrugged uncomfortably.

"Yeah, that's what I thought," Colin said.

"Okay!" Jen said. "I was a jerk. Please, I'm trying to be nice. And I really am sorry."

"And I accept your apology," Colin said, forcibly softening his voice.

"Can we still be friends?" Jen asked.

Colin chewed his lip as he thought about Jen's question. What would Jess do in this situation? He made a snap decision and said, "Yes. But…"

"But what?" Jen asked in a wary tone.

"But you have to not bully Ashley anymore," Colin said.

Jess looked like she wanted to argue at first, but instead she nodded slowly. "Fine."

Colin smiled cheerily. "Let's go dance, shall we?"

He pulled the door open with a whoosh and waited for Jen to walk through it before entering the room himself. Gina caught his eye and gave him a questioning look. He winked and she smiled back. Maybe Jess' friends weren't that bad.

"Ladies," Ms. Valmez said. "This is our last rehearsal. You have all danced so beautifully." Her eyes roved over all the girls standing in rows in front of her. "I am so proud of the progress you've made over the summertime. I wish you all good luck tomorrow. Now," she snapped her fingers, "let's dance!"

They got into position to start their first number. Colin moved with the other girls, taking his time with the slow, graceful moves that Jess had been teaching him. He glanced at the clock in the room. Jess would be getting up soon for her last practice, too. She'd put on his cleats, tall socks, shorts, and t-shirt. She'd comb his hair, because that was something she cared about. Soon, she'd be kicking a ball around with his friends, get yelled at by his coach, and take it all like a man. She was cool that way.

Colin realized with a start that he'd gotten lost in his thoughts, but had not lost one single beat of the music. His steps hadn't faltered and he hadn't missed any of the moves. He smiled to himself. He finally felt like he was getting good at dancing.

As Jess ran back and forth, passing off the soccer ball when needed and blocking it at other times, all she could think about was Colin. She wondered if his dance recital had gone okay. She wondered if he would go out with the girls afterward or if he was still mad at them. She wondered, above all, why Colin had agreed to kiss her and at the last moment pulled away.

Was she supposed to believe that line about Colin not deserving to have Jess' first kiss or something? They hadn't talked about it the night before and now Jess regretted not having brought it up. The whole thing was just so confusing and messed up. Jess took her feelings out on the poor soccer ball heading toward her.

"Nice pass!" Jon called to her, holding his thumb up like a hitchhiker.

"Thanks!" Jess called back.

On top of all that, Colin had been so adamant about Cass not going out with Ian but when Jess asked what they should do, he'd shrugged it off? It was like every time she thought she had him figured out, he did something else to surprise her. Of course, that just meant that Colin was deeper than Jess would have originally given him credit for.

Jess passed the ball to Ian, who then took three long strides forward, aimed, kicked, and scored a goal. Their side cheered loudly.

"Colin!" Ian called from the other side of the field. "You're back in it!"

Jess raised a fist in the air in triumph. It was then that she realized exactly what Ian had said. He thought Colin was back to himself, which obviously meant that Jess was playing well enough to fool Colin's teammates. That was even more cause for celebration in Jess' mind, even if she was preoccupied with everything else.

When the practice was over, the coach came over to Jess and said, "Good hustle, Jacobs."

"Thanks, Coach," Jess said, flashing him a big smile.

Jess then narrowly escaped having to have another conversation with Ian. She knew full well that he was going out with Cass tonight and she didn't need to hear more about it. She jogged home – or rather, back to the Jacobses' house. When she got in, Cass was playing piano again and singing.

Jess invited herself into the den where she was singing. Cass tilted her head toward Jess, signalling that she knew she was there, but to Jess' relief, she didn't stop singing. This song was faster than the last one she'd heard Cass do, and she could tell Cass was struggling with the piano part. But once again, the quality of Cass' singing far outweighed any faults she had.

When Cass was finished the song, she spun around on the stool and Jess clapped for her. Cass smiled and took a little half bow in her sitting position.

"I'm not very good at playing that one," Cass said.

"No, you're not," Jess teased with laughter in her voice. "But your singing is always great."

"What's up with you lately?" Cass asked. "You're being so nice."

"I'm… not," Jess said.

"You are," Cass said. She smiled at her. "Not that I mind too much."

"Yeah, you're right," Jess said. "I'm just in a good mood. Hey, do you want to go out with me for a while?"

Cass hesitated and then said, "Okay… but I can't go out for too long. Because I have a date tonight."

"Yeah," Jess said. "I know."

"You do?" Cass asked in surprise.

"Yeah." *Stupid, stupid, stupid.* "Jess told me," she explained quickly.

"That was nice of her," Cass said insincerely.

"Look, forget I said anything," Jess said, pleading with her eyes. "Let's just hang out for a bit."

"Alright," Cass agreed. "Let me go change."

Jess ended up waiting for about ten minutes for Cass to change. Now she understood from a guy's point of view why it might be slightly annoying to have to wait for a girl to have an outfit change for every event in life. She made a mental note not to do that when she was back in her own body. If she ever got back into her body.

While she waited for Cass, she texted Colin to say, "Going out with Cass. Anything you want me to tell her?"

He texted back immediately with, "Yeah. Tell her she's the princess of light and music."

Jess shook her head. She wanted to ask what exactly that was supposed to mean, but she didn't get a chance. Cass came down the stairs at that moment, grabbed Jess' arm and whipped out the door. Jess let Cass steer then in the direction of the old downtown section of the city. Jess had never actually been there with Cass before, so she wondered if maybe this was something Cass and Colin shared together.

After a while, Jess finally asked, "Where are you taking us?"

"Remember that old toy shop Mom and Dad used to take us to when we were little?" Cass asked.

"Oh, yeah!" Jess said, faking memory of a place she had no knowledge of.

"I just haven't been there in a while," Cass said. "I thought it'd be fun."

"Sure," Jess nodded.

As they perused the old – or creepy-looking, in Jess' opinion – toys, Cass' face took on a nostalgic expression. Jess could tell this place really meant a lot to Cass, and it probably had meant a lot to Colin at one point too.

"What's the deal with you and Jess?" Cass asked out of the blue.

"Um, what's the deal with you and Ian?" Jess asked, not wanting to answer Cass' question.

"We're going out on date," Cass said like this answer should have been obvious.

"Oh, right," Jess said. "Are you sure that's such a good idea?"

"Really, Colin?" Cass asked with an edge of exasperation. "I've already heard this from Jess, okay?"

"You have?" Jess asked. Of course she had. "Well, good."

"Yeah, so don't bother. It's not going to change my mind." Cass gave Jess a condescending pat on the cheek. "Now answer my question."

"What question?" Jess asked nonchalantly, picking up a miniature rocking horse that looked like it was from the 1800s.

"You and Jess," Cass replied.

"Nothing's going on," Jess said hastily.

"Are you sure?" Cass asked as she moved into the next aisle that was full of porcelain dolls.

"Yes, I'm sure." Jess laughed. "What's the big deal, Cass?"

"It just seems like you guys have been hanging out a lot lately," Cass said.

"We've seen each other a couple times," Jess said. "In large groups. With other people around."

"Well, I think I should know if my best friend and my brother are dating, that's all." Cass picked up a doll, and watched her eyes close as she laid it down. "You know, just in case you're sneaking around behind my back."

"We're *not*," Jess said. "I mean, don't you think she would have told you if we were doing anything?"

"Yeah, I guess so," Cass said. "Hey, look at this."

Cass held up a doll dressed like a princess with a wind-up pin at the back of it. Cass wound it up and as soon as she let go of the pin, the doll's face lit up and music started to play. She handed the doll to Jess, who took it gingerly in her hands. Suddenly, Colin's last text came to her mind.

"It's like… a princess of light and music," Jess said, wondering if finding the doll was purely coincidence. She smiled at Cass. "Kind of like you," she added, hoping that didn't sound as weird as it felt to say.

"I was wondering if that's what it would make you think of," Cass said with a grin. "Man, you used to always tell me that story."

"Because you loved it so much." Jess didn't have to guess to know it was the truth.

"Yeah, I did. I *do*," Cass corrected herself.

Jess smiled. Later after they'd gone home, she shut herself in Colin's room and pulled out his cell phone. Colin picked up on the first ring.

"Hey, what's up?" Colin asked.

"Tell me the story," Jess demanded without preamble.

"What story?"

"The story about the princess," Jess said. "And something about light and music."

"Oh… that story."

"Please tell me?"

Colin sighed. "I used to tell Cass this story about these two kids."

"You're an awful storyteller," Jess commented dryly.

"Alright, fine…" Colin took a deep breath to stall for time. "Once upon a time, there were a king and queen in a galaxy far, far away. They were worried because they had no children and were starting to get old. But then, one day a son was born to them, the prince. A year later, they had a daughter. She was the princess of light and music. Happy?"

"So… it's you and Cass," Jess said in an awed voice.

"Well, you certainly caught on quicker than Cass did," Colin said. "Although, granted, she was a lot younger than you are now."

"So, did you make the story up yourself?" Jess asked.

"Yes," Colin answered matter-of-factly. "Cass used to have a lot of trouble getting to sleep when she was little, so I would tell her that story. She kind of fell in love with it."

Jess smiled really big. "Thanks for telling me the story, too. It's cute."

"Thanks," Colin said. "See you later?"

"See you."

SEVENTEEN

"So," Jess said.

"So," Cass answered with a hint of attitude.

"That's what you're going to wear, eh?" Jess asked, looking Cass up and down.

. Cass had chosen to wear her favourite pink, spaghetti-strap dress that fell to just above her knees. She'd topped it off with a sequined jean jacket and added strappy black sandals to the mix. Jess also noticed that Cass was wearing the necklace Jess had bought for her last birthday. Jess was momentarily touched by the gesture.

"What's your problem, Colin?" Cass asked, putting a hand on her hip.

"Nothing," Jess said, feeling slightly guilty. "I was just going to say that you look very pretty."

Cass gave her a sceptical look, but she softened her stance. "Look, I know how you feel about me going out with Ian. I've heard you. But I want to give him a chance."

"I understand," Jess said solemnly.

As soon as Jess watched Cass ride off in the car with Ian and his mom, she called Colin. "Go out with me," she said gruffly when she heard him answer.

"You sure know how to treat a girl," Colin joked.

"I'll come by and get you." Jess almost hung up instantly.

"Whoa," Colin said. "Hold up. Where are we going and why?"

"*La Casa Blanca*," Jess said. "Put something pretty on."

"*Jess*," Colin said, "there's where Cass and Ian are going." He looked at the clock in Jess' room. "In fact, they should be getting there about now."

"Colin, we're going. Get dressed."

"How'd you know I was naked?" Colin quipped. When Jess sighed audibly, he asked, "Look, why do you want to go so badly?"

"Because…" Jess sighed again. "Because you were right, okay? I don't like the idea of her and Ian going out together. So we're going to go… make sure they're okay."

Colin snorted. "No, we're not. But have fun."

"Colin –"

"Do you want her to hate you, too?" Colin blurted out.

"She doesn't hate you," Jess said quietly.

"Yeah, well, she will if she sees you there," he said.

"So, we'll make it like a date."

"What?" Colin squeaked.

"We'll make it –"

"I heard you, thanks," he said. "But that's a little obvious, don't you think?"

"Colin," Jess pleaded. "Please. Please do this with me." When Colin hesitated, she added, "I know you want to."

"Okay," he said after a long silence. "But don't blame me if this all goes wrong."

"You said it yourself; it won't make things worse between you two."

"It's *your* relationship you should be worried about ruining," Colin pointed out. "Okay, come get me."

"Wear something nice."

"Yeah, yeah."

Jess gave Colin a few minutes before heading over to her house, not that she thought Colin would make good use of it. The most awkward moment of Jess' life happened when her father answered the door and took a good long look at her.

He didn't speak and finally Jess said, "Um, I just came for Jess?" like it was a question.

"Colin Jacobs," Mr. Lewis said with a slight upturn of his lips. "I wondered how long it would take you."

"What do you mean, sir?" Jess asked, genuinely confused.

"Oh, I'm sure you've had your eye on her for a while," Mr. Lewis answered. "Well, come in and wait. She's still getting ready."

"Thanks," Jess said softly, stepping inside the house. Her dad thought she and Colin were just waiting for a first date? That was weird.

Colin came down the stairs a few minutes later, and it looked like he had actually taken the time to make Jess pretty. Really pretty, actually. He had put on a nice blue sundress that went well with Jess' blond tresses. He had even put on lip gloss. But his shoulders were bare.

"Hey, Jess," Colin said nonchalantly as he made his way down the stairs.

"How did you...?" Jess couldn't finish her question, but instead let it hang as she gaped at him.

"How did I what?" Colin asked, his brows drawing together.

"Nothing. Put a sweater on," Jess said, recovering from her surprise.

"What? Why?" Colin asked, half on a step, half off.

Jess came closer and said under her breath, "I don't want my parents to see me going out like that."

Colin suppressed the urge to roll his eyes, but went back upstairs to get a sweater anyway. "Can we go now?" he asked when he came back down.

"Yes... they've probably already eaten their appetizers," Jess said impatiently.

"Don't get snippy with me," Colin warned.

"Sorry," Jess muttered.

They stepped outside the house and Jess started walking at a furious pace down the sidewalk. Colin took a few steps and then stopped, crossing his arms across his chest.

"Jess," he called. "We're not walking, are we?"

"Yes," Jess answered over her shoulder.

"Have you ever tried walking in these shoes?" Colin asked.

Jess finally stopped walking and turned around. Looking pointedly at her own black heels, she said, "Yes, actually, I have."

Jess held out her arm for Colin to hold onto and he scurried to catch up to her, the heels clicking sharply. Colin's gait was awkward as he clung to Jess' arm for support. Jess was impatient to get to the restaurant, but she couldn't help the small chuckle that escaped her lips.

"Shut up," Colin muttered.

"Is that any way to treat your very fine date?" Jess teased.

Colin glanced at Jess' clothing choice. She had put on dress pants and a nice polo, but at least she didn't look ready for a funeral. And she hadn't made his hair look stupid today either.

"You look nice," he complimented.

Jess blushed, but she said, "You realize you're just complimenting yourself, right?"

Colin shrugged. "You make me look good, I guess."

"Thanks. You look nice, too, by the way," Jess said. Colin gave her a look, and she smiled. "I mean it. I can tell you took the time to look good."

"Oh please, you always look this good," Colin blurted out.

"You think so?" Jess asked in an awed voice.

"No," Colin said, blushing profusely.

Jess didn't answer, but she couldn't help the little smile on her face. Maybe her dad was right in his assumption after all. She kept her thoughts to herself, though.

By the time they reached *La Casa Blanca*, Colin's feet were killing him. He wanted to whine and complain, but he knew it would be lost on Jess. At the front counter, they were met by a cheery seating hostess.

"For two?" she asked with a wide grin.

"Obviously," Colin muttered.

Jess grabbed his hand, smiled at the hostess, and said, "Yes please."

"I have a table, just by the far corner windows," the girl said, seemingly unfazed.

Colin followed her line of vision and his eyes widened when he saw that Ian and Cass were sitting at the table right next to it. "We don't want that one," he said hastily.

"We don't?" Jess asked.

"No," Colin said, pointing with his chin in Cass' direction.

Jess looked over, pursed her lips and then looked back at the hostess. "Yup. Can't do that table. What about that one over there?" She pointed to another one across the room that had a good view of where Ian and Cass were.

The hostess looked down at her seating chart and shook her head slightly. "I'm sorry, that one's reserved."

"So, switch the tables," Colin said impatiently.

Jess squeezed Colin's hand and smiled politely. "Would it be possible to maybe switch the tables?"

The hostess half-rolled her eyes. "I guess…"

"Great!" Colin said.

As the seating hostess led them toward the table they'd indicated, Jess gave Colin a warning shake of her head and kept his hand in hers. She snuck around, hiding behind other tables, a fake tree, and a waitress carrying two trays of food to avoid being seen by Cass and Ian. Then, hey took the proffered menus and hid behind those as well.

"What do you think they're talking about?" Jess asked, surreptitiously glancing over at Ian and Cass.

"Who cares?" Colin asked, scanning the menu. "I'm starving. You're paying, right?"

Jess let out an exasperated breath. "Fine, whatever. But don't forget why we're here."

Colin perused the menu for a few minutes and then asked, "Is she flirting a lot?"

"So, you *do* care?" Jess threw at him.

"Just answer the question. You have a better vantage point."

"What exactly do you consider flirting?" Jess said, tilting her head around her menu to see better.

"*Jess...*"

"Okay, yes, she's flirting with him. But, what did you expect? They're on a date together."

"Is she having a good time?"

"I'd say."

"Is he maintaining eye contact?"

"Colin, I can't see that far. Why don't you just go over there and find out for yourself?" Jess asked.

As soon as Jess said the words, she regretted them. Colin started to stand, and then Jess tried to pull him back down to his seat. Instead he ended up in her lap. After staring at each with startled eyes for about two seconds, Colin bolted upright.

"This is so, so very wrong," Colin said, dropping back into his seat and covering his face with his hands.

"Oh no."

"*Oh no?* What oh no?"

"He saw us," Jess whispered frantically.

"Who?" Colin whispered back. "Ian?"

"Yes." Jess turned her head away from the direction Ian and Cass were sitting. "Just ignore them. Maybe he didn't recognize us."

"Didn't recognize his best friend?" Colin asked sceptically.

"Oh, you're right," Jess said. "Cass will probably see us too, and there's no mistaking a best friend *and* a brother." She glanced over once more and a grimace crossed her face.

"Did they see us?" Colin asked, concern finally creeping into his voice.

The look on Jess' face was answer enough. Colin half-turned in his seat and glanced over at them briefly. Cass and Ian were looking right at them. Cass shook her head with an angry glare as Ian waved at them in a friendly gesture. Jess and Colin looked back at each other with grim faces.

"They know," Jess said soberly.

"What do you want to do?" Colin asked.

"Let's just leave," she said softly.

"Okay, let's go." Colin got up to leave, feeling Cass' eyes still on him, but desperately trying to avoid her.

Jess got up to make a hasty exit with Colin, but just as she'd pushed her chair in, Ian called to them. "Col! Buddy!"

Jess gave Colin an apologetic look and turned slowly to face Ian. He was smiling like a goof-ball and waving them over. Ignoring the warning look on Cass' face, Jess started toward them.

"Jess," Colin hissed, grabbing her arm to stop her.

"Colin," Jess said quietly so no one would hear them using each other names, "we're going to have to explain ourselves sooner or later. We might as well just get it over with."

"She'll hate us," Colin reminded Jess.

"I think she already does," Jess said in defeat.

Colin let go of Jess' arm and resignedly followed Jess to Cass and Ian's table. Ian was blissfully unaware of the tension passing between the other three, and it made Colin almost grateful that Ian was his best friend. If it weren't for Ian's excitement at seeing them there, they would all be awkwardly staring at each other in this half-angry atmosphere.

"Dude," Ian was saying, trying to give Jess a high five. Even though Jess didn't respond, he said, "Sweet, a double date. Come on, grab some chairs."

Jess swallowed hard and looked right into Cass' eyes, a sort of question passing between them. Cass' jaw was clenched and she was visibly angry but she shrugged in a way that Jess knew meant, "You're here now, why not sit down, jerk?"

"Actually, we should probably go," Colin said, apologetically eyeing Cass.

"No, please. Sit," Cass said, giving them both icy stares.

Both Jess and Colin hesitated so long that Ian finally got up and grabbed two chairs from a nearby table. They sat boy-girl, boy-girl at the little square table, and Jess couldn't have felt worse in that moment that she'd managed to conjure up a hatred for her and Colin in Cass.

"We can't stay long though," Jess said.

Cass crossed her arms in front of her as Ian said, "That's okay. It's cool you guys are here. Why didn't you tell me, dude?"

"Yeah, Colin," Cass piped up. "Why didn't you tell anyone?"

Jess half-shrugged as Colin answered, "It was a spur of the moment thing."

"Oh yeah?" Cass asked in mock interest. "Which moment was it that you decided to come here? Was it three days ago when I told you *I* was coming here?"

"It wasn't like that, Cass," Jess tried to say.

"Really, we only decided to come here like an hour ago," Colin confirmed.

"Yeah, like I really believe that," Cass spit out.

"Whoa, whoa," Ian cut in. "What's going on here?"

"Nothing," Colin and Jess answered together in a tone that clearly said something *was* going on.

"What's going on," Cass answered, finally turning to face her date, "is that Colin and Jess decided to come and check out our date tonight."

"I don't understand," Ian said, his jovial attitude finally slipping.

Cass opened her mouth to say something, but Colin spoke up before she had the chance. "Colin, let's just go."

Jess nodded and stood to go. "I'm sorry, Cass," she whispered before joining the quickly-retreating Colin.

Cass just shook her head and glared at them until they had left the restaurant.

Jess and Colin started their walk home in a tense silence. Neither one of them wanted to talk about what had just happened. The worst part of it was that Ian had been nothing but nice to both of them all week, up to and including his date tonight. And they hadn't even bothered to give him the benefit of a doubt. Halfway through their walk, Colin leaned down and pulled off Jess' heels.

"What are you doing?" Jess asked. "You're going to walk without shoes on?"

"I hate these stupid shoes!" Colin burst out. "I don't want to walk around in your stupid shoes, or your stupid clothes, or your stupid makeup! I don't want to be inside your stupid body anymore!"

Colin's outburst startled Jess into a stunned silence. Finally, she said in an icy voice, "Do you think I like this? Do you think I want to pretend I like soccer for everyone's benefit but my own? Do you think I enjoy dressing in your shabby clothing and having my best friend ignore me half the time?"

"Well, great," Colin said. "Now you know how I feel. It's not so great being me, is it?"

"Colin, you are *such* a martyr," she said, shaking her head. "I mean, do you have any idea what you sounded like just now?"

"Not that it's any better being you," Colin continued, not wanting to own up to what she was saying. "Your friends think you're a child. Your parents practically forget that they birthed you. I would almost take being ignored by Cass just so I don't have to listen to her anymore!"

Jess clenched her fists and kept up to Colin's shoeless, fast-walking pace. "Is that your problem? People are suddenly paying attention to you because they think you're me, and you just can't handle it because you don't want people to see what you're really like?"

"What is that supposed to mean?" Colin asked angrily.

"It means 'look at me! I'm Colin and I push everyone away because I don't want anyone to get too close to me,'" Jess answered, sounding equally as angry.

"Look at me!" Colin yelled, throwing his hands up in the air. "I'm Jess and I don't need to push people away because they already don't want to be near me."

Jess stopped walking and just stared at Colin's back. He'd gone too far, but in a moment of weakness, she wondered if maybe Colin was right. Well, she didn't want to stick around to find out. She turned and started walking down another street.

When Colin realized Jess wasn't next to him anymore, he stopped and looked around him. "Jess?" he called quietly. "Where'd you go?"

He backtracked, looked one way and then the other, and finally saw Jess practically jogging down another street. "Hey!" Colin called. "Okay, I didn't mean it! I'm sorry."

Jess turned around but kept walking backwards. "You don't want to be near me, then fine! Leave me alone." She continued on her walk.

"I said I was sorry," Colin said, sounding anything but apologetic.

Jess stopped, turned once more, and pinned Colin with the angriest look she'd ever given anyone. "You call yourself a Christian, Colin, but do you even have any idea how to actually be one?"

Colin stopped following Jess and just gaped at her. If he were to be honest with himself, he'd say that his behaviour in the last ten minutes wasn't very Christian. But his male pride prevented him from actually admitting that. Instead, he kept his mouth shut and watched Jess walk away from him. It was only when she was out of his sight that Colin finally decided to make his way to Jess' house.

EIGHTEEN

"Are you happy?" Cass yelled outside of Colin's bedroom door.

After her argument with Colin, Jess had stalked all the way to the Jacobses' house, gone to Colin's room, and slammed the door shut. She'd been waiting there for a couple of hours when she heard Cass come home. But now that Cass was home, Jess was reluctant to come out of the room.

Cass didn't have any more to say, however. After her outburst, she quickly slammed her own door shut, making Jess jump at the sharp sound. She knew she shouldn't have been surprised, but she was hoping Cass might have cooled off by the time she got home.

Jess gave her another half an hour to brood in her room while she prepared what she would say. When she was finally ready, she went and knocked on Cass' door. There was loud music coming from her room and no immediate answer following, so she knocked again, this time louder.

"What?" Cass called from inside.

"Can we talk?" Jess tried calling over the music.

Cass opened up the door with a whoosh and asked, "Haven't you done enough?"

"Cass, please," Jess said softly. "Can I just come in?"

"No," Cass said defiantly. "You can say what you have to say from out there."

Mustering as much Colin-like confidence as Jess could, she moved past Cass' slight body into her bedroom anyway. She wouldn't allow Cass to treat her like an outsider, not when Cass thought Jess was her own brother.

"You always just do whatever you want anyway, don't you, Colin?" Cass shot a glare at Jess.

"Look, Cass," Jess started to say, "I'm really sor –"

"Oh please," Cass cut in. "Don't. Just don't. You ruined my date. Ian thinks I'm an idiot. No amount of apologizing can fix any of that now."

"Please just listen to me," Jess said. She was encouraged when Cass remained silent. "Jess and I were just... concerned for you. We just wanted to make sure you'd be alright."

"Oh," Cass said. "I see. Well that makes it all better."

"Really?" Jess asked disbelievingly.

"No!" Cass exclaimed, throwing her hands up in the air. "What were you thinking? That one little explanation would really make me any less mad?"

"No," Jess said. "I just wanted you to know that... we just care about you. Okay?"

"I'm a big girl, Col," Cass said tightly. "I don't know how you managed to get Jess to go out there with you tonight, and I honestly don't know what's been going on between you two lately. But you both should have known better."

Jess took a deep breath. She knew that she'd screwed things up for Colin by doing this, and she could only hope that she could make it better right now. So she said, "It was Jess' idea."

"What?" Cass asked.

"It was her idea to go," Jess said evenly. At least it wasn't a lie.

"With absolutely none of your input?" Cass asked.

Jess shut her eyes tightly and then opened them again. "Look, Ian hasn't exactly always been boyfriend material, if you ask me. I've seen him make enough girls cry to know that I didn't want the same for you." Jess might have stretched the truth a bit, but it sounded close enough to what Colin had told her and what she had seen of Ian herself. "I might have mentioned something like that to Jess."

"Why wouldn't you have just come to me?" Cass was hurt, Jess could tell, but she wasn't completely innocent in this either.

"I tried, Cass," Jess argued. "You didn't listen. You just did what you wanted."

"So, I guess we're not that different after all," Cass said in an icy tone.

"I guess not," Jess said. "I really am sorry that I ruined your date."

"Yeah well," Cass paused and looked away from Jess' eyes, "you got what you wanted in the end. There's no way Ian's going to ask me for a second date now."

"What happened after we left?" Jess only wished she could have asked that as herself, not as Colin.

Cass shook her head. "I'm not talking about that with you."

"Will you with Jess?"

"What?"

"Will you ever talk to her again?" Jess asked. "Would you forgive at least one of us?"

Cass was silent for several moments and she wouldn't meet Jess' eyes. Finally she said, "It would take a lot to get me there."

"I understand," Jess said sadly. "Goodnight, Cass."

"Are you going to go to her recital tomorrow?" Cass asked as Jess was stepping out of her room.

"Why do you ask?" Jess asked curiously.

"It just seemed like you two were getting really close," Cass replied. "So, I thought you'd want to go. That's all."

Jess shook her head. "I think the try-outs will overlap too long for me to make it." She paused and then asked, "Are you going?"

Cass sighed. "I promised her a long time ago that I would."

"It would mean a lot to her," Jess said, feeling slightly encouraged.

"I know that," Cass snapped. "Remember, she was my best friend before she was anything to you."

"I know," Jess said quietly. "I'm sorry."

With that, Jess left Cass' room and trudged softly back to Colin's. Colin was right, after all. They never should have gone. She'd single-handedly ruined Cass' relationship with Colin, Ian, and herself, not to mention her own tenuous relationship with Colin.

The only thing she could do now was prepare herself for tomorrow's try-outs and play the very best she could. She knew that she would never be as good as Colin, but she owed it to him to try. Even if he was too mad at her to perform her recital.

After a sleepless night, Jess rose the next day feeling groggy and out-of-sorts. But despite that, she got up, ate a hearty breakfast, and went through some stretches and practice kicks in the Jacobses' backyard. After lunch, she got dressed for the big soccer practice. The try-outs were at 2 p.m. and the recital was at 3 p.m.

Around one o'clock, Jess hurried over to her own house, completely dressed in soccer gear, but not caring who saw. If she was going to get to Colin, she'd have to make it quick in order to make it to the soccer field in time.

She thought about going through the front door, but that would be suspicious. So she made her way to the backyard and surveyed the back of the house. If Colin could climb up to his own bedroom, she could certainly climb up to hers. It was awkward, but with the help of some tree branches, a drainage pipe, and cleats against a brick wall, she made it.

Not bothering to knock first, she opened the window and climbed inside. As soon as Colin heard her, he whirled around. And that's when Jess realized she'd walked in on Colin getting dressed. And by the looks of it, he was getting ready to dance.

"Well, this is kind of awkward," Jess said, openly staring at her own half-naked body.

Colin blushed, despite the fact that he realized that Jess knew what her own body looked like. Ignoring her comment, he pulled the closest material to him over the front of him and asked, "What are you doing here, Jess?"

"Well, I came here to see if there was any chance that I could get you to go to my recital," Jess explained. "But it looks like I didn't really need to do that. Here." She handed Colin the top half of the outfit that was lying on the bed.

Colin pulled the shirt over his head and then said, "A deal is a deal." He sent an appreciative look at his soccer uniform.

"Colin, I wanted to…" Jess hesitated. "I wanted to help you get ready. And maybe do your makeup so you don't look like a tramp."

Colin rolled his eyes, but he handed her the makeup kit and sat down on the bed. Jess started pulling out some eye shadow, blush and mascara.

"I also wanted to apologize," Jess said as she dipped a brush in some heavy foundation. "You were right. We shouldn't have gone last night."

"Cass was pretty mad, wasn't she?" Colin asked.

"Yeah, she pretty much hates my – your – our guts," Jess said. A humourless laugh escaped her lips. "I think she might come see you dance, though." Colin nodded, but didn't say anything.

"I was awful to you," Jess added a minute later. "And I'm really sorry for that. Because you're the only person who understands what I'm going through right now. And if I can't be nice to you, then I'll have no one to support and to support me."

"I was pretty horrible, too," Colin said softly. "I'm sorry. And I'm glad you're here. Because right before you came through the window, I was taking your costume off."

"You were?" Jess asked in surprise.

"Please don't be mad," Colin said. "It's just that… this whole thing is so crazy, you know? And then I thought after last night, you'd be too mad to do my try-outs, so why should I bother dancing?"

"I see," Jess said disappointedly.

"But then you showed up in my uniform and…" Colin shrugged. "I am a horrible person, aren't I?"

"You're not," Jess said. She paused to put some eyeliner on Colin. "After today, you can quit."

"Quit what?" Colin asked.

"Quit dancing," Jess said in a low voice. "You won't have to do it anymore. You can even join another sport, if you want. Just… please break it to my parents gently. Believe it or not, they've put a lot of money and as much effort into my dancing as I have."

To Jess' great surprise, she saw tears appear in Colin's eyes. "In that case," he said, "you might as well not go to try-outs. 'Cause you don't have to play soccer after this."

"I'll still go," Jess promised. "A deal is a deal, right? Plus, soccer isn't that bad. I could live with it."

"I can't ask for that," Colin said.

"You're not," Jess said, her voice quavering a bit. "I'm offering."

Colin nodded. "I'm going to dance well for you."

A tear slipped down Colin's cheek and Jess could feel her own eyes brimming with unshed tears. "I know you will. Now don't cry. Your mascara will run."

Colin laughed. "You don't either. Soccer players don't do that."

Jess joined into his sad laughter. With a tissue, she wiped Colin's cheeks where the tear had run and finished up her makeup job. "There. I have to go, or I'll be late."

"Thanks, Jess," Colin said. "Good luck."

Jess couldn't help it. She pulled Colin in for a tight hug. "Good luck to you, too."

NINETEEN

Colin warmed up and stretched with the other girls. He tried not to let all his feelings show. He knew if he thought about his and Jess' conversation, he would start to cry again and he'd promised Jess he wouldn't ruin her makeup job. On top of that, he was nervous about the recital. He couldn't even think about the try-outs, even though he knew they were currently happening.

"Hey, Jess," Gina tapped Colin on the shoulder. "Someone's at the door for you."

"Oh," Colin said in confusion. "Okay…"

He went to the backstage door of the theatre and when he opened it, Cass was standing on the other side. Colin stepped outside the warm-up room and shut the door softly behind him.

"Cass. Hey," he said.

"Hey," Cass said quietly. Her face was drawn tight, but the fact that she was here was a miracle in itself.

"I'm really sorry about last night," Colin said. "That was really stupid."

"Yeah, it was," Cass said, but there was no resentment in her voice. "Colin told me… it was your idea."

That threw Colin. It *had* been Jess' idea originally. But of course, Cass thought he was Jess, so it made sense. Sort of. "Yeah, it kind of was. But if it's any consolation, I do regret it."

"He said you were concerned for me," Cass said. "I just wanted to know why."

Colin hesitated. He hadn't expected this conversation to come so soon. "I guess I didn't trust Ian. But… He's not that bad, after all."

"He was extremely gracious after you two left last night," Cass said. "But I felt like an idiot."

"I know, and I really am sorry," Colin repeated. "What can I do to make it up to you?"

"I don't know yet," Cass said cautiously.

"I understand," Colin said. "Are you going to watch the recital?"

"Well, I didn't pass up Colin's try-outs just to talk," Cass said. Then she gave Colin a small smile.

"Thanks, Cass," Colin said, returning his smile. "I really appreciate it."

"Colin said you would," Cass said. Colin put his hand on the door handle, but Cass said, "And Jess?"

"Yeah?"

"If there is something going on between you and Colin," Cass paused, "that's okay with me."

Colin didn't know whether to say thanks or deny everything completely. Instead, he nodded and said, "I'll catch you later."

"First string!" Coach called, tossing Jess a temporary jersey that would later be replaced with one that read 'Jacobs' across the back.

Jess grinned, proudly hugging the jersey to her chest. "Thanks, Coach."

Coach handed an identical jersey to Ian and Jess smiled at him. "Congrats," Ian said, holding up his jersey.

Jess stepped closer to him and said, "You, too. Looks like we'll be playing together after all." She wasn't sure yet whether she meant it, but she knew she owed it to Colin to make things right with Ian. "Thanks for helping out, Ian."

"No problem," Ian said quietly.

"Listen, about last night..."

"Yeah, I'm sorry, dude," Ian said.

"Wait... what?" Jess said, completely confused.

"I'm sorry, that whole thing was weird," Ian said. "I thought you and Jess were on a date. I didn't realize..."

"That we were keeping tabs on you and Cass?" Jess finished, before Ian got the completely wrong idea.

"I didn't realize you thought you needed to," Ian said. He looked down at his shoes.

"Look, I'm the one who should apologize," Jess said, touching his shoulder. "You're my friend and I handled that really badly. I'm sorry."

"It's alright, Col," Ian said. "But you're right, I'm your friend. Even though you should have said something, I know I've given you plenty of reason to be worried."

"I didn't mean it that way," Jess said softly.

"I know," Ian said. "But hey, for what it's worth, I really do like Cass. I never would have hurt her. But now... I think she's too embarrassed to even consider a second date with me."

Jess bit her lip in thought. "You know what, Ian? She likes you, too. I'll talk to her, okay?"

Ian's face lit up with a wide smile. "Really? You'd do that?"

"Yeah," Jess said with a smile. "And I promise I won't mess it up."

"She's at Jess' recital right now, isn't she?" Ian asked.

"Yeah," Jess said with an enthusiastic nod.

"Then what are you still doing here?" Ian gave Jess a teasing smile.

Jess laughed and started running away from the field, ignoring the rest of Colin's teammates and friends as they tried to congratulate her.

She just wanted to get to the theatre to see Colin as soon as possible. She couldn't wait to see the look on his face when she told him. Jess ran hard for almost ten minutes until she reached the theatre.

She caught her breath outside of the building, and then slipped in silently. The screen was lit in soft blue, and a new number was just starting. Jess recognized the dance as soon as the first chords started. She watched the girls take slow, graceful steps out onto the stage from both sides. The side on the left was led by Colin.

Jess caught her breath as she watched the girls dance. They were all lyrical, poetic, classy. Colin, especially, danced his part perfectly. Every move was just right, every line, every arch, every point of his toes. He looked... beautiful to Jess.

A sadness swept over Jess, as she suddenly remembered that this was her recital that she was watching. That she had just won the first string position for Colin. She got up and left the hall as quietly and quickly as she'd come and made her way back to the soccer field.

The field was empty now, with only traces and remnants of the previous match that had been played to determine positions. Jess sat down on the bottom row of one of the bleachers. As she looked out at the field, she recalled the feeling of exhilaration that she'd had while playing. Soccer really wasn't that bad once she got used to it.

Jess sat outside alone for a long time, losing track of everything. The recital had long ago finished. She was startled out of her reverie by a light tapping on her shoulder. She looked up. It was Colin, wearing a huge grin. She smiled back.

"I did it, Jess," Colin said excitedly. "I danced and didn't fall or do something stupid."

"I know," Jess said softly. "I saw some of it. You were... you were perfect."

"How come you didn't stay?" Colin asked. He gazed into Jess' softly frowning face. "Hey, is there something I should know about?"

"Yup," Jess said. "I made first string."

"Really?" Colin squealed. "Wow, Jess! I'm so proud of you. That's great!"

But something was still wrong that Colin couldn't put his finger on. Then he looked down at Jess, who was still dressed in his soccer uniform. He had actually gone back to Jess' house to change before coming out to look for her. He slouched down into the seat next to her, and sighed.

"What now, Colin?" Jess asked. She stood up and started pacing. "Do we start school as each other on Tuesday?"

"We can still figure something out," Colin said unconvincingly.

But Jess wasn't listening. "How long can we keep this charade going?"

Colin didn't have an answer. He didn't have any more solutions, and he'd run out of ideas. His only option was to submit to what was. "You know, Jess, if I have to be stuck in this body... that wouldn't be the worst thing in the world."

Jess nodded slowly. "Yeah, I feel the same way." But even though she'd spoken the words, the tears gleaming in her eyes belied her true feelings.

"Hey," Colin said softly. "It'll be okay." He stood up and came closer to her. "Here, give Jessie a hug."

Jess made a little sound that was a cross between a sob and a giggle and came willingly into Colin's open arms. As soon as Jess put her arms around Colin's slender shoulders, a spark flew between them, forcing them both backwards.

Jess groaned and stood up, asking, "What was that?" She reached her hand down to help Colin up and suddenly realized... it was Colin! It was really Colin on the ground across from her. "Colin!"

"Jess?" He said wearily, his eyelids fluttering open.

"Colin?" Jess asked, concerned that he might have been hurt.

"Jess!" Colin shouted gleefully. He jumped to his feet, looked down inside the front of his shorts and laughed heartily. Looking up at the sky, he shouted, "Thank you!"

"Look at us!" Jess exclaimed. "I can't believe this. All we had to do was hug?"

Colin laughed again. "I don't think that was quite it, Jess."

Jess laughed along with him. "I know. But still… this just feels so great. Man, I can't wait to get home and see my folks."

Jess turned and started jogging away from the field, but Colin called her back. "What is it, Colin?" she asked.

"We… never finished our hug," he said shyly.

She smiled and came back to him. He opened his arms – *his* arms – once again and wrapped them around Jess. She put her arms around his waist and leaned her head against his chest. Finally, everything felt right. Everything felt okay again.

"Want me to walk you home?" Colin asked, finally releasing Jess from his arms.

"You know what?" Jess smiled up at him. "Yes. I really do. It might help make me feel like a girl again."

"Kind of weird, eh?" Colin asked. He found a stray soccer ball near the bleachers and kicked it ahead of him as they started walking home.

"Yeah, a little bit," Jess said. Glancing down at his feet, she added, "But clearly you're readjusting just fine."

Colin chuckled. "I just missed it."

They walked in a companionable silence for a long time, but the silence was neither tense nor secretive. Finally, they could be themselves again. And on top of that, Jess had won Colin a spot on the soccer team and Colin had danced Jess' recital perfectly.

But still, Colin thought there was something else he needed to say. "I'm sorry I'm such a jerk a lot of the time," he blurted out.

Jess glanced up at him and away again. "You're not," she said softly. "I've misjudged you for a long time. And I'm sorry about that."

"Then all is forgiven between us," Colin said solemnly.

Jess nodded. "Good." She paused and then added, "But you were wrong about one thing, Colin."

"What's that?"

"It wouldn't have been the worst thing ever if you'd been my first kiss," Jess admitted.

Colin didn't answer, but a smile spread across his face with an accompanying blush. Of course, Jess couldn't meet his eyes, so she missed his expression. The silence stretched out between them again until Jess sighed.

"Wow, I can't even get a kiss with an open invitation," she said half-jokingly.

"I've never…" The rest of Colin's sentence drifted off on a murmur.

"What?" Jess asked.

Colin stopped walking, turned to her and, staring her straight in the eye, repeated, "I've never… kissed anyone either. It would have been a first for me, too."

"Really?" Jess asked incredulously. For some reason, she thought Colin would have already passed that landmark in his life.

"Yeah, I know," Colin said. "I'm sure Ian's kissed lots of girls. Just like David Beckham, right? Except, Beckham's married now… but Sidney Crosby's not, and he probably gets kissed all the time."

"Colin," Jess interrupted his rant. "Would you just shut up and kiss me?"

With a shy smile, Colin leaned forward. But just before his lips touched hers, he whispered, "Are you sure you wouldn't rather be kissed by someone with ocean blue eyes and hair the colour of sunshine on a summer day?"

Without a word, Jess put her hands around Colin's neck and pulled him closer until they were kissing, all teasing and thoughts of blue eyes abandoned. They kissed a few more times before finally pulling apart from each other.

"I can't believe you know about that," Jess said, shaking her head with a smile.

"Oh, well, you know girls share all their secrets," Colin answered, flicking his wrist with flair.

Jess laughed and took his hand to move it out of her face. When she didn't let it go, he threaded his fingers through hers and squeezed lightly.

"Well, now I feel kind of bad for Mrs. Abernathy's granddaughter," Jess said.

Colin laughed out loud. "Don't. She's eleven, she'll get over it."

"She's eleven?" Jess asked incredulously. Then she, too, laughed. "I kind of got the impression that she was older than that."

"Yeah, Mrs. Abernathy has a way of distorting things in her mind," Colin said gently. "You'd like her granddaughter though. She's a sweet girl."

"I doubt I'll ever meet her," Jess said.

"You could if you came with us on Sunday," Colin suggested with a shrug.

Jess thought about it silently for a moment. Cass had already asked her a hundred times, she might as well say yes at least once. "Okay," Jess said. "I'll come."

They had reached Jess' house and finally Colin released his hold on Jess' hand. She smiled at him and he grinned back.

"You're a cool girl, Jess," he said.

"You're not bad yourself, Col," she answered.

"I will forever remember this as the summer I turned into a girl," Colin said with a smirk.

Jess reached for the door to her own house and added, "Well it can't be as bad as suddenly being in the body of my best friend's brother."

"Let's never talk about this again," Colin said.

"Good idea."

EPILOGUE

The doorbell at the Jacobses' house chimed and Colin grinned. Jess was joining him, Cass and Ian for movie night. Colin and Ian had argued back and forth with Cass and Jess about what movie to watch, but of course they'd settled on a stupid chick flick. But it didn't matter. Colin was himself and Jess was herself, which almost didn't seem to matter anymore because they spent so much time together anyway.

Colin answered the door and greeted Jess with a quick kiss on the lips. Her blush made him smile. He led her into the living room, where everything was already set up for the movie.

"Where are Cass and Ian?" Jess asked, settling in next to Colin.

Colin put his arm around Jess and answered, "They're getting the popcorn."

Almost as soon as he'd said it, the sound of popping drifted toward them with the smell of hot butter accompanying it. Jess smiled up at Colin.

"Hey, Cass, can I have –?" Ian's voice drifted toward Colin and Jess, the end of his question cut off by the sound of more vicious popping.

They heard the sound of a drawer scraping open as Cass said, "Sure, what do you need it for?"

"Oh, there's something stuck in your toaster," Ian said nonchalantly.

Jess and Colin looked at each other with startled eyes and they both jumped off the couch at the exact same moment. They ran into the kitchen just in time to watch Cass holding the toaster in place for Ian who was just about to stick a fork into it.

"NO!" Colin and Jess cried at the same time.

Cass looked back at them with a frown. "What's with you guys?"

"Got it!" Ian said, completely ignorant of everything else going on. He triumphantly held up a piece of burnt toast. "Hey guys," he greeted with an easy grin.

"Jess, Col… you guys are like completely white," Cass noted. "What's wrong?"

"Don't you realize how dangerous that is?" Jess asked.

"You could get hurt," Colin informed them.

"Or die," Jess added.

"Or worse!" Colin exclaimed.

"What are you talking about?" Cass asked, pulling the toaster in front of her to show them. "It's not even plugged in." She dragged the cord across the counter until it fell, swinging from the toaster.

"Yup, totally safe," Ian said, holding up his burnt toast.

"Plus it hasn't even been working for weeks," Cass said.

"Well's that's probably why," Ian said, waving the fork in her face. Cass' face crinkled into an adoring smile.

Colin chuckled nervously. "Oh… right. Well…"

"Yeah, that was silly, right?" Jess said giving Colin a meaningful look.

"We should probably just throw the toaster out," Colin told Cass.

"And never talk about it again," Jess added.

"You guys are, like, the weirdest couple ever," Cass said, shaking her head in amusement.

"You have no idea," Colin said, giving his sister a smile. Cass smiled back and giggled. Cass would never know. And that was okay with him and Jess.

NATASJA EBY

Natasja was born and raised in Bowmanville, Ontario. Her passion for writing stems from her childhood when she and her sister would make up stories together. She spends a lot of time at the local library, dreaming of the day her books are side-by-side with the classics, and writes indie songs in her spare time.

Made in the USA
Middletown, DE
08 October 2018